PERI ELIZABETH SCOTT

EVERNIGHT PUBLISHING ®

www.evernightpublishing.com

PERI ELIZABETH SCOTT

THE TATTERED BRIDE

Peri Elizabeth Scott

Copyright © 2016

Prologue

12:00 noon

He trailed his tongue up her calf and behind her knee, the strangest sweet spot ever, but Victoria loved that Logan had discovered it. When he left it behind, she was squirming against the sheets, alternately begging him to stop and pleading with him to do it more. More.

Nipping at her thigh, he palmed a buttock. "Such a nice ass, Miss Sparrow. I'll be thinking of this peach tonight."

"Enough thinking, more doing," she grumbled.

"Ah, ah, ah. You know I won't be rushed." He kissed her other cheek, his tongue making a sneaky little foray to tease her senses.

She tried to turn over, but he foiled her effort by lowering his weight across her legs and setting a firm hand in the small of her back. "We'll get to the other side, baby. Patience."

Patience was most definitely not a virtue. Not today. Their wedding was in several hours and she needed to get her hair and nails done, rush to her mom's

5

and get into her dress, and—

"Oh, my God." He'd somehow worked one of those big hands between her thighs and put two fingers up inside her.

"Do I have your attention now?"

"Y … es." It came out all wobbly as she tried to work against those digits. His sexual acumen had woken a passionate wench inside of her she hadn't known existed.

"Good." He pulled out and slid off her in a single movement, flipping her to her back in the next. And then he was between her thighs, his dark hair such a contrast to her pale skin.

She took handfuls of that silky hair, writhing as he laved her tender parts, working that devious tongue high inside her opening. Her thighs fell wider and she arched in a mute plea. Changing tactics, he settled his attention on her aching clit, a finger replacing his tongue.

As he fit deep in her passage, finding a spot he'd hunted out with great deliberation the first time they'd made love, he sucked hard on her clit. A near-scream burst free, past her lips, as dark spots and lights clouded her vision and she spiraled from a hard-hitting climax.

His face damp from her exertions, Logan surged up her body and fit his cock in exactly the right place. He thrust hard, battling for territory against swollen tissues and seated himself with a satisfied grunt. Staring at him, her hands slid along his sides to rest on his firm ass. She wondered how she'd found favor with this man who had the world and most of the women in it at his fingertips.

"God, I love you, Victoria."

"That's the position you're in talking," she teased, though finding words was an effort. He filled her so full and she craved him, precisely in this way.

"Oh, this too. But I love everything about you."

He shifted to work his hands beneath her shoulders, and his cock swelled inside of her.

"I love you right back, Logan Doherty." Soon, she'd be Mrs. Logan Doherty. Victoria Doherty.

Holding her close, he rocked his hips and murmured endearments, his thrusts increasing in intensity. With a shudder, he stilled, his face a study in pained pleasure. She stroked his neck and shoulders as he sagged against her, his cock pulsing.

"I'm too heavy." He rolled off and collapsed against the pillows, taking her hand.

She reveled in the continued closeness, inhaling the dark, earthy scent of sex, and then marked the time. "Logan. I have to go!"

He levered up onto one elbow and kissed her nose. "I guess I can wait a few hours."

"It'll be more than that, you animal." She sat up and slipped from the bed, avoiding his reach. "We have to get ready, and then there's the wedding and the reception."

"And *then* the honeymoon. Or at least our wedding night." He scowled. "I'm sorry we have to delay the honeymoon, baby."

"Your father deems business supreme, Logan. I know. And we'll be going away the end of the month. Something to anticipate." Besides, nearly every day was a honeymoon with Logan. She hustled to the bathroom and quickly showered. She didn't have to worry about makeup or her hair at least, and the salon would do a quick wax of important parts.

When she emerged, he was still sprawled on the bed, and she scanned his languid body. Well, not *everything* was languid. She tore her stare away and searched for her clothes.

Slipping into some fresh underwear, she dropped

a sundress over her head. Logan watched every move. When she stepped into her sandals, he said, "Come kiss me goodbye."

"It's bad luck," she teased.

"It's bad luck to see your bride on the wedding day, and I saw every inch of you. Don't put any stock in that old tale. Come kiss me."

"Promise you won't prolong things? Seriously, Logan. I have to pick up my sisters and meet Kaitlyn and Theresa at the salon. And I haven't had my coffee!"

"You had something better."

"Maybe." She flashed him a smile and he uncoiled his length from the bed, prowling toward her like a big cat.

Laughing, she fended him off. "Teasing. It was a great substitute. Better than great. But I have to go."

He yanked her against his chest, and she breathed in his man sweat, a scent uniquely Logan's. Her belly swooped, but she reined herself in. They had the rest of their lives together. Tipping her head back, she accepted his kiss and bit his lip when he would have extended it.

Releasing her with a wince, he chased her to the doorway, smacking her ass with a mock growl. "You're beautiful enough, but go try to improve on it. I'll see you"—he pantomimed looking at a watch on his naked, muscular forearm—"in a few short hours. And try getting away from me then."

"Deal." She threw him a kiss and raced out the door, not daring to look back. Nearly dancing out to her car, she smiled widely and wished everyone near and far the happiness she felt.

Chapter One

4:00 PM

"Baby, I know the timing sucks. I couldn't have chosen a worse time. I know that. But…"

"What's wrong, Logan? What is it?" The cold chill of dreadful premonition traced its icy finger along her spine. Her own hands clenched around her bouquet, despite her need to touch him.

He winced. The fit of his tuxedo was impeccable, and she watched the jacket tighten as his big body tensed. "There's no other way to say it. I'm sorry. I'm calling off the wedding. We aren't getting married."

The world narrowed to him and her, and a little slice of churning emotions she couldn't decipher. "You're calling off the wedding. Our wedding. Now." Just in case she hadn't heard him correctly. This had the makings of a horrible, sick joke…

Shoving a hand through his hair, he obviously struggled to meet her stare. His tawny eyes were turbulent. "I am. I … just decided. It's—"

"What?" Victoria tumbled to it, falling into the abyss of her history. Deep down, she knew why. Too bad he'd only *just* decided. Now. At this inopportune time. All her issues and stupid insecurities washed over her from wherever they'd been banished to, banished by Logan's resolute pursuit and sincere belief in her. He'd addressed her fears, made her whole—and now? Now her tender underbelly was exposed—without a shred of armor—for the deathblow. The sublime lovemaking of a mere few hours earlier faded in the face of it.

"I—" Real pain and misery now seemed to burn in his eyes, and despite her terrified anticipation, she wanted to soothe him. Through set lips, he continued, "I don't have the words to tell you why Victoria. I'm sorry. But the wedding is off."

Still, she waited, believing he would somehow embellish, give her an explanation that wouldn't make this about her, but he stood there mutely, now staring someplace over her shoulder. She checked out the direction of that gaze—maybe there was an answer there, but she saw only a watercolor of a pastoral scene. *Please.*

She let her pride crumble and begged. "Logan. This doesn't make any sense. We… Only this morning…"

He shook his head and straightened to his full height. "It's off."

Deep inside there was an utter certainty that it did indeed make sense. He'd figured her out. Seen to the core of her the way others had. In despair, she gave up the fight to believe in him and their love in response to his firm declaration. The Victoria of her childhood emerged, in blind response, lashing out to hide from the truth.

"Was it the thrill of the chase? And then when you caught me, you became afraid you were settling? That there's something better around the corner?"

She didn't want to wait for a response. She had to leave. Now. What would get her past the sideways looks and the knowing stares? The church was full of family and friends—and others who had probably predicted this very moment…

"Victoria. You need to calm down. It's not like that."

"Calm. Down?" She was aware her voice was climbing as she talked over him, and the small room, the one where she and Logan would have been closeted to sign the papers finalizing their marriage, wasn't soundproof. She modulated her tone the very best she could, humiliation and pain squeezing her very being. "What *is* it like, then, exactly?"

"I can't say."

"Tell me."

He looked away. "I can't."

Dropping her beautiful bouquet of red roses, entwined with baby's breath and white, embossed ribbon on the desk, the air currents disturbed the uncompleted marriage papers. They fluttered, mocking her. She stared up at the face of the man she loved. And faced the realization that she indeed still loved him. That part, at least, hadn't changed despite the mortification of being dumped at the freaking altar. *Love.* She thought it was love. Too bad it wasn't real.

"And I'm supposed to take that and be calm!"

"Yes, calm down." His face was set in grim determination, his eyes hot. "We'll … we'll get through this."

She narrowed her eyes and leaned into him. What couldn't she be one of those classy women who took this kind of thing in stride and walked away without making a scene? Maybe she could be. Drawing on a reserve of strength she wasn't aware she possessed, she said, "I'm calm. Dead calm. So shut up now. I never want to hear your voice again, let alone set eyes on you."

Squaring her shoulders, she closed off his next attempt to speak. She avoided his outstretched hand and ignored the sudden abject despair written across his handsome features. Was he embarrassed? If he didn't want a scene, why in hell had he chosen this public place to dump her? Flinging the door open to the main part of the church, she surveyed the people filling the pews. Those congregated there stilled into silence, with only an occasional murmur marring the quiet. Dozens of pairs of eyes looked in their direction. Victoria stepped forward. Classy. She could do this.

Logan was behind her—close enough to feel his heat—and the familiarity of it made her falter. Probably that very familiarity was what had palled. For him. The thought of losing him... She dug deep. The time to fall apart was later. Much later. If ever. Resolutely, she faced forward and spoke, projecting her voice into the corners of the vast space.

"I'm sorry you all came out today. There will be no wedding. I'll see to it that your generous and thoughtful gifts are returned. Thank you."

A swell of whispers and a few louder voices echoed and battered her ears, and she flinched. Logan placed a hand low on her back, but the touch no longer felt supportive or possessive, two sensations that had always thrilled her. Instead, it burned her very soul, because it was a mockery—and a reminder—of what they'd had.

She jerked away, and marched, as best as a woman swathed in the wedding dress of her dreams could march, past the altar, where her four bridesmaids waited, and the worried-looking minister. Past the groom's family, vaguely marking the snide twist on old man Doherty's lips and the tears on Logan's mom's face. Past her horrified family, sans her father, of course, her mother scrambling up to follow. Her sisters abandoned their posts beside the minister to contain their children who were squealing with delight to see her, and her brothers-in-law frowned thunderclouds of destruction toward Logan.

"Auntie!" Little Patricia struggled in her mom's arms, her flower girl's finery awry. "Come see me."

Victoria forced a smile and a wave before hustling to the door. If Logan trailed her, she didn't care to know, holding it together with the last of her composure. She focused straight ahead and somehow managed not to view the sea of faces lining the aisle.

"Tori." Her mother's anguished tone had her slowing to let her mom catch up. Together, they walked, side by side, not at all in the way Victoria had moved with her mom toward Logan, who'd been waiting for her beside the minister, flanked by his best friends, David and Patrick, and her brothers-in-law, Robert and Michael. Was that only a few minutes ago? The recollection of that hope, the anticipation and breath-stealing euphoria sucked the life from her as they crashed and burned forever.

"I need to get out of here. Is there a car we can use?" She discounted the limo at the curb, its tasteful 'Just Married' sign surrounded by more red roses and ribbon.

"Frank's is over there. He never locks it and hides a key. We'll take it."

Bless the woman beside her, in that she didn't pepper Victoria with questions, giving her the immediate privacy she so badly needed to get to those four wheels denoting her escape. Although where would she go that she wouldn't take herself?

When had she suspected the instant her future was in shambles? It had been Logan's inscrutable—blank—face, she decided, as he took her hand from her mom's, his fingers curling so firmly. There had been a dire warning there, belied by the warmth of his touch. Not the proud, soon-to-be-groom she expected, with appreciation and admiration—and love—written large across his gorgeous features. And then he'd escorted her into that little room, the entire church speculating. So why had she even allowed herself a smidgen of hope?

He'd swept her off her feet from the first, tearing

down her defensive walls, softening her heart, gaining her trust, making her believe she could love him with all of her soul. He was such an amazing man. She'd opened herself up to him…

Her heart skipped a beat as the air squeezed from her lungs, and it wasn't the tight corset impeding her breathing. How far was the damn car? When she spotted the silver sedan drawn tight against the curb, she shuddered. Stumbling the last several feet, she sprawled into the passenger seat. Her mom shut the door, after making a half-hearted attempt to shove the material of Victoria's wedding dress inside. Her veil tugged, caught in something, and she worked it out of her hair, squishing the netting with its beautifully applied pearls into an ungainly wad of fabric.

Her mother slipped into the driver's seat and fumbled at the visor. A key fob dropped and a small hand, tipped with pink varnish caught it, and then rammed it into the ignition. The motor caught and with a slam of the shifter, the vehicle rolled away. Victoria let down the window and tossed out her veil, watching in the side mirror as it unfurled, catching an updraft before drifting to settle on the street. Ruined and so defenseless.

She supposed it would get run over by countless vehicles, torn and trashed beneath unrelenting tires until it was unrecognizable. Kind of like her heart. Leaning back on the head rest, she reached up to free the remaining pins securing her fancy up-do. Her long hair tumbled down, easing the massive headache settling in to grind against her temples. She let it swing forward to screen her face.

"What happened?" There was a limit to her mother's patience, and it occurred that maybe people thought Victoria had derailed the wedding. He hadn't added his voice to hers when she made the announcement, and for an instant, she clung to the idea that she could put it about that *she* had stopped the proceedings. But her innate honesty put a stop to that. She wasn't going to be responsible for concocting a story.

Maybe using some succinct words would wrap it up and give her the opportunity to practice what she'd say to everyone else who asked. "Logan told me he couldn't go through with the marriage."

"Why?"

"He didn't say." *I couldn't bear to hear his excuses, anyhow, that it was about him, not me.* Because that was what he'd have come up with, had she stayed. She knew it. He might have hurt her terribly with his rejection, but the Logan she knew wouldn't have made it about her. Except she knew the truth, and why should he have to lie? It wouldn't have changed anything or made her feel better.

Victoria recognized the unvarnished truth about herself despite what other people said. The trauma of early years scarred deep, and for her, obviously lasted a lifetime. She'd been stupid to believe anything Logan said. Nothing was forever, except for maybe the survivors' bond within her family.

The tires whirred against the uneven pavement and some country and western tune on the radio whined quietly in the background. Why couldn't they sing about trucks and horses instead of hearts? Broken ones. With shredded souls.

"He didn't say. O … kay. You weren't curious to know why?" Despite her calm tone, Victoria could hear her mother's pain, once she'd processed the information.

"Sorry, he *wouldn't* say. But whatever. I already know. What's the point in him skirting the issue? And … I was overwhelmed. I mean, he couldn't have told me before? Someplace a little less public? I was right there, Mom! Right fucking there, fifteen minutes away from being married. In front of everyone, like the worst kind of movie. You'd just given me to him. G ... given me." She swallowed against nausea, pretending the loss wasn't real. Better she found out ahead of time, right?

"I'd like to kill him. Slowly." Her mom was always in her corner.

"I'm not talking about him anymore. Okay? I need to get past this and move on."

"Tori, you can't shove your relationship with Logan into some tidy little sack and tuck it away, like ... like you've done with upsetting things all your life. It's too big. You love him. He's your life. There has to be an explanation."

Maybe her mom could find a really sharp knife and open her up with it too. Check her entrails and forecast the future. Sucking in a draught of air between her teeth, she formulated a reply. "All true, Mom. All of it. And look where it got me. I've got such fantastic judgment, despite what I know about men, huh?"

"Not all men," her mother responded. "But you could sue him. Breach of promise. Hit him where it hurts, right in the wallet." Her mother was now dissolving into chaos too.

She'd win any such lawsuit. She'd seen it in Logan's eyes. He felt bad for leaving her at the altar, because he was a good man at heart, even if she wasn't in it any longer. He'd throw money at the problem. This time, the nausea was intolerable and she gagged. Her mother shoved a wad of tissues at her.

"We're soon home."

True to her word, they pulled into her mother's driveway and right up to the house. The sight of her childhood home broke that something deep within

Victoria, and she sobbed into the tissues. It should have been a refuge, but only served to remind her of another man, another rejection.

Tears welled, too numerous to hold back, and poured down her cheeks. The tissues couldn't contain it all. Ducking her head, she watched as her makeup swirled and mixed with the moisture to drip free and soil the pristine white of her wedding finery. Murky gray mascara, tinted with foundation, was the final shade of her life.

She might have sat inside Frank's car for an eternity, sinking into that awful muddle of color, but her mom came around to yank open the door and urge her out.

"C'mon. Let's get you inside and out of … that." *That* was probably an apt descriptor of the dress she'd chosen with such care and attention to detail. Not too sexy, not too poufy, not too prom-like. Just right. To marry the wrong guy. Correction. To be thrown over by the right guy.

She couldn't see past her tears, despite swiping at them to clear her vision. Careless of dragging her bridal gown across the greasy door mechanism, she clambered out, one heel tangling and tearing the hem. The tattered bride. Oops, the tattered bride-to-be. Not. Maybe it was something she could think on for the magazine, kind of a play on marriage, complete with pictures and personal experience.

Laughter bubbled up and she choked on it, staggering behind her mother's diminutive form. The heel caught in the hem gave her a curious gait, reminiscent of that strange little man in the western movies her dad favored years ago. The additional memory of her father drove her to her knees, and she wavered there, swathed in pain and bridal white.

Wrenching off her heels, she waved away her mother's help.

"I'm okay. Just off balance." The understatement called up the laughter again.

"C'mon. Get up. Leave the shoes." Her mom's face was so creased with worry it added a decade to her appearance.

The neighborhood was silent. They were probably all at the church. She clambered to her feet and tossed the heels at the recycling bin, laughing harder. Getting through the doorway into the back vestibule felt surreal, and her impromptu merriment ran down like a depleted battery.

With help, she divested herself of the gown, leaving it in a crumpled mass on the kitchen floor. She stood, in her corset and tap pants, in her thigh highs with their wide band of sexy lace, and shivered. Here she was, half naked in her mother's kitchen, instead of basking in the lustful gaze of her husband on her wedding night.

There would be some of her old things in a closet. Her mom wasn't a hoarder, but she unerringly kept things her daughters needed. "I'll go change into something."

"There's some items that'll fit in the dresser in the spare room. Closet too, I think. I'll make tea?"

"Okay." She was vastly fatigued and that one word took incredible effort.

The short trek to the spare room—Juliana's old room, the oldest girl—took forever, as though she was relearning how to walk. She wobbled and banged into the walls. Once inside, she doffed the corset and stockings, consigning them to the trash. Unearthing a light sweater in the dresser and a pair of leggings she was sure had been around since the nineties, she pulled them on. They mostly fit, and were as comfortable as an old shoe.

Shoes. She refused to give in to the hysteria bubbling through her chest.

Logan's ring winked up at her as she smoothed the leggings over her thighs and she froze, staring at the beautiful canary diamond set with green tourmalines. Large enough to be noticed, but not ostentatious. He knew her well and understood she'd balk at an ice cube. *He knew her well.* She was close enough to the narrow bed to catch her weight on the edge of the mattress as she sagged.

Logan had come to know her so well he didn't want to spend the rest of his life with her. Clever man. She was hardly Logan Doherty wife material, after all. Oh, she was pretty enough, some might even say beautiful when she made the effort, with her thick, dark hair and pale skin with contrasting dark-blue eyes. She was tall and had a good body. She'd heard it all her life. The prettiest Sparrow girl, built like a brick shithouse. Not that it meant much in the end.

And not that she traded on it. If anything, good looks got in the way of someone in the cutthroat advertising business. At twenty-eight, she'd been accused of sleeping her way to the top over the years, and people tended to get stuck looking at her instead of seeing who was behind the façade. Logan had looked behind it and said he loved the whole package.

Indicated he was in awe of her drive while appreciating her ability to see the bigger picture and care for the little guy. She'd felt worshipped, special, like she'd finally moved past the crippling misery of her childhood and arrived in the company of a wonderful, trustworthy man.

He'd said a lot of things, all of them now suspect, and she blessed the fact she hadn't quit her job and joined his firm when he'd asked her to, so many times.

"Tori?" Her mom stood in the doorway, watching her warily.

She caught sight of herself in the mirror on the dresser and realized her mom had reason to be a tad cautious. Tangled hair and smeared makeup aside, it was the look on her face... With an effort, she wiped the desolate expression away. "Tea ready?"

Her mom held out the phone. "You should take this."

"Who is it?"

"Logan's mother. Delores."

Air whooshed out of her chest and she nearly doubled over. Her voice squeaked as she replied. "Uh, no."

"She wants to explain something."

"Logan's a big boy, Mom. His mommy doesn't need to hold his hand."

"Maybe she's trying to hold yours."

"I have a mother." Victoria liked Delores a great deal, and a shred of remorse lingered, but surely she was entitled to establishing boundaries, at least while she recovered. There. She'd already decided there was the potential for recovery.

With a nod, her mom turned and went down the hall, murmuring into the phone, while Victoria choked back a sob. How did one recover from having one's heart ripped, live and beating, from one's chest and sliced into irreparable pieces in front of one's eyes?

Tired of the drama, she tugged off her engagement ring and tossed it at the garbage can. It clipped the rim and ricocheted off, plinking against the wall before hitting the floor someplace. She fingered the lovely earrings her future mother-in-law had given her, and removed them, setting them on the nightstand. No doubt her mom would get them back to Delores. If not, she'd have then couriered, but the two older women had really hit it off, despite their very different social spheres. So, in all likelihood, they'd get together if only to discuss the almost marriage.

Leaving the fine chain with the perfect pearl around her neck—a gift from her own mother, and one that had probably broken the bank—she shoved to her feet and shuffled into the bathroom.

Scrubbing her face clean with a handy cloth, she then ran her fingers through her hair and bundled it at the nape of her neck, wrapping the long strands around to secure it, all the while avoiding the mirror. She made her way back to the kitchen, where her mom was still on the phone. There was no sign of her dress and she experienced not one iota of interest in its whereabouts.

"I'll tell her, Delores. I'm sure she'll call once she's had a little time." Her mom locked stares with her before concluding the conversation and laying the phone down. "Come sit."

Victoria snagged the phone before taking her place at the small bistro table that saved the kitchen from being overcrowded. Her purse was—someplace else. Probably one of her bridesmaids would have it. She ignored the hope on her mom's face and dialed a number from memory. As she predicted, Jonathon was already back at his desk. He'd probably left the church right after her announcement and driven straight there. He worked more hours than even her and Logan, and would find his job a way to deal with his worry until he saw her next.

"Jon?"

Her mother stiffened and the tea she was pouring slopped into the saucer.

"Victoria! What the fuck? Are you okay? I've been trying to call you."

"I'm fine." Probably a lot of people were trying to call her, so not having her phone was a good thing. She sucked in a deep breath. Time to practice. "Logan decided he couldn't go through with the marriage." There, that didn't hurt at all. The truth didn't hurt. It flayed and tortured.

"I can't believe that."

"Believe it. He blew me off."

"Jesus. I'm sorry, sweetie. That bastard." Her boss thought Logan Doherty was one of the hottest slices of manhood on the face of the planet, but his loyalty was to her and it was a tiny balm on the painful pandemonium in her chest.

"Gave me an idea for an advert, Jon. It'll appeal to a wide variety of users. We might as well capitalize on the publicity."

Silence. Jonathon King was never silent. She waited and wondered if maybe she'd lost her mind, but then he cleared his throat. "You never cease to amaze me. Would it be therapeutic maybe, Tori? Help you out a bit?"

"Definitely."

"Then get your ass in here. We'll get started."

"An hour," she promised, glad he understood her need. When the going got tough, Victoria Sparrow immersed herself in her work. But first, she had to get to her house and change clothes after having a cup of tea with her mom.

She powered down the phone and nodded her thanks for the beverage. One sugar flavored the deep amber of the orange pekoe, a favorite of her Gran's. The teacups had belonged to her grandmother too, and the nostalgia couldn't hurt. A sip, followed by another, eased her aching throat and soothed her belly, if not doing a thing for that vast hole in her heart. Her Gran said a good cup of tea could fix anything. Maybe she should make a bathtub full and drown herself in it.

"You're going to stuff it down, after all. You won't talk about it and it'll mark you. You'll carry it the way you did your father's rejection until it impacts the rest of your life." Her mother's voice reminded her of reality.

"Mom, I'm gutted. I won't pretend to you. And I'm pretty sure I'm aware of how this will impact my life because I'm destroyed. Devastated. Okay? I'm not hiding from it. But please don't play therapist and compare Logan to Daddy." She gulped some tea. "Sadly, a small part of me isn't surprised. He cut a swathe amongst the ladies for a decade or more, and why would he settle for me?" *For the likes of me.* "But I'm not going to hide and dwell on it. What's the point?"

And she wasn't going to let it slip to her mom that she accepted there was no real reason for Logan to change for her when *he* wasn't damaged. Because then her loving parent would adopt that therapist persona again *and* be tortured with guilt.

Her mother rested a hand over hers, and the warmth was comforting. "He loves you, Tori. There's an explanation. I know it. Delores really wants you to call her. Please."

"Look. I just went through one of a woman's worst nightmares. I don't want to hear her try to comfort me. Make excuses for her son's behavior." Delores had lucked out, losing Victoria as a daughter-in-law.

"You think I don't know how that feels, Victoria? That I don't remember?"

"Sorry, Mom. Really." She knew her dad walking out had gutted her mom too. Hadn't he told her she should have given him a son? Like it was *her* fault? And then Victoria had lived with the culpability of not being a boy child for more years than she could count, the shame staining her psyche. No matter how her mother tried to reassure her differently. It had shaped her. Wrecked her as a person. She'd never felt good enough, and hid that lack behind blind ambition and hard work. Relationships with men—even boys—always ended the same way. On their terms, because she was so afraid to commit. Until Logan.

"I know, lamb. I know you are. But I know *why* your father left—no matter how stupid the reason—and it helps. Because it was about him and not us."

She didn't want to hear trumped-up excuses. Not when she knew the truth. She tried to deflect. "What could anyone say that would explain that last-minute dumping? All those guests…"

She would have to think about the logistics, and it would be her cleaning things up because she no longer trusted her ex. Ex. Her thoughts jumbled again.

"Delores said they were all invited to attend the reception—well, not the reception exactly, but the food was there and…" Her mom trailed off and hid her face in her cup.

Was there additional mortification to heap on a person? Maybe so. Victoria savagely hoped Logan choked on the meal they'd chosen so carefully and decided she no longer cared who returned the gifts. Maybe those attending the "reception" could receive an invitation to his condo to pick them up. He could assign them time frames to avoid overcrowding and make them produce a sales slip to ensure they took the item they'd purchased. But, for her mother, she was pragmatic. "Well, his father insisted on the damn thing being so huge. All-inclusive, I believe he said, like we'd leave out someone important to his view of the world. I suppose there's no point in wasting all that money."

The old man had picked up the tab because she couldn't, and her mother certainly couldn't, and Logan's parents insisted. The pseudo-reception would now give everyone a chance to mingle and speculate and gossip about the called-off wedding, and maybe solve the crisis of the fucking environment and the world's other problems too.

Drawing on the anger, which was a welcome singular emotion to focus on, she drained her cup. "Thanks, Mom. I'm heading back to my place." And thank God she'd kept her house, despite Logan's pressuring her to move in with him before the wedding.

She had her job and her own space. No husband, but hey, a person couldn't have everything. Her mom was giving her that wary look again, so she forced a smile. "Did you want to drop me off and return Frank's car? Maybe he's at the reception."

"Victoria. Stop. Your family won't have gone there. Nor will your true friends."

Shame lanced through the anger. Frank wasn't exactly family, but he was her mom's kinda significant other, on and off, since her dad left, and she hoped he caught a ride with someone. Maybe one of her sisters.

"Sorry. Of course, they wouldn't. Too bad, though, what with all the party favors. The kids would have loved them." She wasn't tracking so well now but knew getting to the office would help a lot.

"I'll drive you to your place, though I think a bottle of whiskey and my company would be a better bet." Her mom's voice was a little chilly.

"I'd be asleep after two shots, Mom." Which was likely her mother's plan, but she couldn't sleep her life away. She had decades and decades ahead of her, and the next few weeks would be the absolute worst, dealing with both kind and not-so-kind comments. That was why this burgeoning tattered bride advertising project was becoming so important. It would build on her personal tragedy while putting a different spin on it.

The phone buzzed and a familiar number danced across the screen. The desperate lie she'd been weaving unraveled and spots and lines wavered in front of her eyes. She shoved the device toward her mother who clearly debated answering before tapping the answer button.

"I have no idea where my daughter is, Logan. She's not here and I know she's not at her house." Victoria could hear his deep voice, though refused to try and decipher the words. "I'll let her know you called." She pressed the off button and set her lips.

Victoria breathed a sigh of relief. "You used to cover for me with my less reputable friends, Mom. Give me a way out when I couldn't seem to stand up to them. Thank you for this."

"I didn't lie, Tori. I really don't have any idea where my daughter is. But I hope she finds herself soon. I'll be here when she needs me."

Left to ponder that cryptic statement, she followed her mom out to Frank's car in a pair of gardening clogs, and they drove in silence to her place. She could sense her mom's … not exactly disapproval, maybe disappointed acceptance, but she couldn't drum up anything to assuage her. If she had to focus on the enormity of what had happened as if it had actually happened to her personally, Victoria figured she'd probably fade into nothing. Better she created a fantasy and distanced it. *Like you told everyone your dad had joined the space program and couldn't live at home. And then surpassed yourself in your studies to graduate ahead of everyone else, the better to avoid them.*

She shoved that memory away, along with the little voice. She'd been a kid, pretending her life was normal and would get back on track. She wasn't going to lie to herself this time, merely twist the situation, and hey, make it work for her. As an adult, she had the power.

Big sister Juliana, and Victoria's nephew and niece were crouched alongside the flower bed skirting her tiny cottage, ostensibly pulling weeds. Her sister levered to her feet and rushed the car, pulling Victoria into a tight hug as she emerged. She'd taken off her matron-of-honor dress at some point and changed into jeans and a t-shirt.

"What an asshole."

"Maybe *I* called it off." She hugged her sister tight and refused to cry.

"As if." Juliana leaned back and looked up into Victoria's eyes. "You didn't, did you?"

"No. Logan decided he didn't want to get married." A slight variation, but still practice. It still fucking hurt. She had to make it so it would feel as though it had happened to someone else. Desensitizing, she thought it was called, itching to get to the office.

"Why not?"

"She has no idea and isn't inclined to find out. She thinks she's figured out the reason on her own." Their mom updated Juliana and cuddled Mikey and Sabrina close when they milled around Victoria's legs. "Where's Paige and the kids?"

"Had to go home. Too much excitement. You know how Murphy gets without a nap. Robert and Michael decided to stay out of the line of fire, and went golfing in their suits. Straight to the course. It was that or they were going to hunt Logan down and have it out with him."

Victoria blessed the fact she had such a wonderful family. Her brothers-in-law would indeed chase Logan down at a word from her but would defer to the first line of defence—her mom and sisters. She loved her nieces and nephews too, and seeing as she'd never have any of her own—

The truth smacked her in the face. There would never be anyone else in her life. Not only because she'd never trust another man, but because her heart belonged forever to one Logan Doherty. Never mind he'd ripped it from her chest to crumple and shred it. A faint sound escaped her and Juliana stepped in for another hug, this time patting Victoria's back in one of those soothing motions she used on her kids when they were struggling or thwarted.

"It'll be okay, Tori. It will."

Mikey and Sabrina were staring at them, and her niece's bottom lip was trembling. Oh, no. No. Logan wasn't going to impact her family any further. He was not. Victoria stood tall once again, gently disengaging from Juliana. It would be okay. It had to be. She focused on Sabrina.

"Hey, Sunshine."

The little girl hesitantly moved toward her. She still wore her bridal party dress, now stained with dirt and grass.

"Did you pull out all of Auntie's nasty weeds?"

"Where's your princess dress? And your crown?" The child's eyes were huge.

Victoria's hand lifted involuntarily to where her pseudo tiara had secured her veil. She supposed it was in the gutter too, and that brought tears to her eyes. She'd loved that tiara, having chosen it with her nieces' help. "Sorry, Sabrina. I'm not going to be a princess after all."

"But, Auntie! Logan's your prince! I like him."

"The prince forgot the shoe, Sabby. I can't become a princess without a glass slipper." She stuck her foot out to display the pink clog.

"Huh." Her sweet niece puffed up with outrage as predicted, her anxiety displaced. "I liked the paper-bagged princess better anyhow."

Juliana gave a startled snort of laughter at the reference to the childhood book, and Victoria heard their mom gasp. Out of the mouths of babes, etcetera. Victoria should have identified with that gem or something, but instead, she fought against crushing sadness. With an effort, she smoothed Sabrina's hair, her hand trembling. "Right. Me too."

"Here's your purse. Your keys and phone are inside. I thought you'd need them."

"Thanks, sis."

"Logan has lit your phone up. And a ton of others. I didn't answer, just silenced the thing. Kaitlyn and Theresa send their love and want to take you out to get smashed."

Her best friends were her sisters, but Kate and Theresa were good people. She simply couldn't deal with their way of addressing tragedy. "I'll call them later."

"We brought your car back too." Juliana gestured behind the house.

"Thank you. I'll need it. I'm going into work." Her ability to think clearly had no doubt been compromised, but she needed the distraction—badly.

"I figured you might. That's what I told the guys and Paige. Moving on, right?" At Victoria's shrug, she continued, "You come by tonight and we'll talk. Paige will be there. Mom, you come too. We need to give Tori a little time before an intervention."

"It seems my role's been usurped." Their mother's tone was wry but also full of acceptance. "If that's what will help…"

Kissing her sister and mother on the cheek, Victoria ruffled the kids' hair and hurried into her place, the house key cooperating despite her icy fingers. She left her purse on the table and rushed to the bedroom, tearing off the borrowed clothes as she went. After fumbling into a bra, she chose a pair of tight jeans and a casual shirt and then stepped into a pair of flats.

A lick of makeup very nearly hid her pallor and empty eyes, and she added some colorful earrings to brighten her look. She checked her phone and the number of calls and texts were staggering. Her bridesmaids had called, and Jon, as he'd said. A few others were numbers she didn't recognize, but a vast amount were from Logan.

Grabbing a jacket, she snagged her purse, worried she was working against a deadline. Logan now clearly had thought of something to say—an explanation—but she wasn't listening. There was nothing he *could* say. She'd meant what she'd said. Never. Again. In fact, she'd stop on the way to the office and get a new number and a new phone for good measure.

When she arrived at her place of work, clutching her new smartphone in a stupidly pink case in one hand and a tray of lattes in another, Jon was pacing. He rushed to relieve her of her burden, carefully setting the coffees down before wrapping her up in a hug. She was going to break into pieces if people kept this up.

"How are you?"

"If you quit asking me, I'll let you have one of the lattes."

"Oh. Right. I'll stop." He peered into her face, his blue eyes nearly as dark as her own, and with thicker lashes. Jon was too pretty for a man, but it suited him, and he played it up with an exquisite taste in clothing and expensive haircuts.

"I'm bursting with ideas. You ready?"

"As ever. Though I should tell you Logan called." He held up a hand at her start. "I didn't tell him you were coming. Just that you weren't here. What could he possibly want? He didn't get a chance to jilt you thoroughly enough?"

"Jilt?" Victoria hadn't heard that word—in ever. She didn't think.

"You know. Rejected. Abandoned. Spurned."

Each word arrowed straight through her spurious defense and she grabbed for a latte to hide behind. "I like spurned the best. Spurned." If she said it three times fast it didn't sting.

"What?"

"As the title of our spread. 'Spurned: The Tattered Bride'. Jilted doesn't have the same effect. It sounds more like a jousting tournament or something." And listen to her, being all lighthearted and funny.

"If you're sure, Tori."

Was she? Did she have a choice? "Lemons and lemonade, Jon. I appear to have a shitload."

"There's no chance he's rethought it? Wants you back?"

"And I should take him back, if that were even possible? Trust a man who might as well have slayed me?" It should have sounded terribly dramatic, but it rang so truthful Jon's face fell.

"No. Trust is the basis for any relationship, sweetie. I just thought…"

"I know. Everybody hopes for that happily ever after." Except for her and the paper-bagged princess. Who had the healthier attitude?

"Well, if you're here to work, let's have at it."

****

"She's out there, but I have no idea where."
Logan fought the urge not to hurl his phone at the wall of windows gracing his large corner unit. "And she must have a new number. I can't even get her voicemail anymore."

"She wouldn't give you a chance to explain?"

"What was I supposed to tell her, Mom? He has me over a barrel. Until I can figure a way around his machinations, I'm stuck. When he showed up at the church and dropped the bombshell, I knew he'd go through with it, that everything was in place and nothing I could do would stop it unless I called off the wedding right then and there. He flashed his phone, all ready to send that text."

And it went without saying that as the absolute pinnacle of humiliation for the woman Sean Doherty didn't want his son to marry, the old man couldn't have timed it better. The bastard had slipped into his seat just as Victoria came up the aisle, looking so beautiful and hopeful that the dichotomy of the situation ripped something deep inside Logan. And for once in his life, he'd been immobilized until the warmth of her hand in his spurred him into action. The only private place had been that little room, and trying to find the words...

He pressed a hand over his eyes. He hadn't been able to manufacture even the shoddiest excuse, because no justification would have been true.

The largesse in inviting the entire congregation back to consume the reception food and drink had been a master stroke by the old man too. Even if Logan could have talked Victoria into giving him a chance, to wait for an explanation at a later date when it wouldn't matter that she found out the truth, facing all those people would be daunting. Memories were very long. And Victoria was so damn sensitive when it came to men. He had labored intensely to gain her trust and had been forced to break it today. The idea of patricide flitted in and out of his thoughts as his mother spoke again.

"I called her mother," his mom said. "All she could tell me is that Victoria nearly collapsed, but then she rallied and is moving in some new direction. I could tell it upset Margaret."

Fuck. It upset *him*, and that was putting it mildly. His woman was strong—and resilient. But he knew her personal history. The look in her eyes when he'd called off their wedding and hadn't explained why—there was no point in tormenting himself in the daytime. He'd have enough nightmares to keep him company, and he'd be sleeping alone. Whatever Victoria was embarking on wouldn't bode well for their relationship. He snorted. What relationship? He'd destroyed that with a few words. Or lack of them.

The sight of her veil lying in the street, a forlorn drift of fabric barely anchored by the delicate tiara she'd picked in honor of all the little princesses in their lives, would haunt him forever. It hadn't withstood the big tires of the limo taking his father to the reception, nor the other vehicles that followed. Logan thought his chest would crack open when he'd retrieved only the bent and battered headpiece, the veil beyond repair.

"I'll haunt her place tonight, Mom. She has to go home sometime, and I have a key." Although, with his father, it stood to reason that he'd have Victoria followed, the better to ensure Logan wasn't reneging. So, he'd be careful. "In the meantime, I'll start deconstructing my crazy sire's masterpiece."

"He's like Machiavelli. Or … or a bloated spider with a twisted web. And he's had a long time to perfect the art. I'm sure he's steps ahead, Logan. I don't understand why he disapproves of Victoria."

"He wants me to make an *upwardly mobile marriage*."

"Look where that got *him*," she said, bitterness flavoring her tone.

"It got me one of the best mothers around. And Jackson, and Evelyn, and Christina."

"I love you too, Logan. In case I don't tell you often enough. As for your siblings, you need to tell them what their father did. Let them help you. They were flabbergasted today."

"I can't. You know that was one of his conditions. No one else is to know but him and me, or he'll blow us all out of the water. And Jackson would take his head off without slowing down to think. As for my sisters… Well, they might think on it for a couple of minutes before doing the right thing, but there are thousands of other people out there counting on me. I broke his rules bringing you in on it, but I know he can't read you and you'll never let on."

"So you'll give up your chance at happiness for the stockholders?"

"And for our staff, the clients, my family. Victoria will understand once I've dealt with it and tell her." She had to. Of course she would. His girl never put herself first, so he'd made sure to assume that role until…

"You should have told her up front," his mother fretted.

He kicked a chair, and it skidded across the polished hardwood, bumping into the coffee table where a slender figurine wobbled. Logan sprinted to catch it. Victoria had left only tiny imprints in his home if one overlooked the spare room crammed to the brim with wedding gifts, but the crafted figure he rescued was one of them. Anything of hers was carefully chosen and definitely meaningful.

Taking a deep breath, he answered, "Victoria couldn't have hidden her reaction from the old man today if it meant saving the universe. He'd have known we were merely postponing the marriage. He set us up perfectly and I had to avoid telling her anything." *And drive her away.*

"He's a bastard. He'll go straight to hell." Tears clogged her voice and she sniffled.

Logan wasn't sure he believed in hell, but the old man deserved to burn there if anybody did. "Gotta go, Mom. I have everything here I need." Except Victoria. "And Dad will never know I'm suborning him. I'm far better at this than he is." He hoped. The problem was, it would take time, and that was a luxury he couldn't afford regarding Victoria.

"Good luck, son. I'm here if you need me. Any time. And I'll keep in contact with Margaret, and try to keep the connection."

Carefully setting down the figurine, his fingertips feathering the long, smooth body, he made his way to his study, a pretentious name for a home office, but one the Doherty family used since he was a kid. All the files he required were on a couple of thumb drives his PA had spirited from the office.

While his father was squatting in the church like a malignant demon, ready to unleash his own particular brand of hellfire on unsuspecting people if his youngest son didn't toe the line, Logan had gotten word to Elaine. The woman had slipped from the church, right after Victoria, like a master of undercover stealth to perform the theft, and he'd be forever grateful to her.

Chapter Two

"I'm seeing two of everything." Jon rubbed at his eyes, then his chest. "And that take-out food is talking back."

"The result is good enough that I don't mind seeing double." Victoria surveyed the layout with bone deep satisfaction—and something else she refused to define. It was sheltered by the numbness at her core.

"It freaking well is, honey. Any ideas of who we'll get for the model?"

Someone polar opposite to me. She didn't voice the instant response, smothering it with a gulp of cold latte. At least she wasn't suffering from the after effects of Thai, being unable to choke any down. With a grimace, she set the cup away and pretended to speculate. "Medium height, blonde over brown—or gray, ethereal."

"That would work." Jon hadn't asked again if she was certain she could do this, though she hadn't missed the sideways glances as they'd toiled on the layout.

But she'd maintained her work demeanor, intent and focused, and he'd partnered her with that eerie connection they had. He might be the boss, but he loved to do this kind of work, a hobby to give him a break from his real position. Maybe she should marry Jon, seeing as they could finish one another's sentences, and they never really tangled. And cheating wouldn't be a big issue, seeing as he batted for the other team. A bitter lance of humor made her lips twitch.

"What? I don't see a thing funny here, Victoria. Profound sadness, and lots of darkness, despite the blank face." He frowned at her, perfectly coiffed hair ruffled, his tie unknotted.

She yawned to cover the ghastly smile. "Tired unto death, Jon. Nothing funny. What time is it?"

"Nearly four in the damn morning."

Her wedding had been scheduled for twelve hours earlier—she batted the thought away. "No wonder we're tired."

"And I have a breakfast date at ten." He waggled his eyebrows. "He plays tennis."

"Then head out and get a few hours, my friend. You have bags under your eyes and your date deserves a well-rested match."

"*You* have holes where your eyes should be."

"Nice. So good for a girl's self-esteem." She laced her tone with as much sarcasm as she could muster, and Jon lifted a hand in apology.

"You're going home too, right?" he asked.

"In a bit." She'd canceled the intervention at her sister's last night, making the call from the ladies' room. A good thing, because Juliana's reaction had been epic. Both her sisters, never mind her mother, had threatened to come straight down to the office and drag her home. It was only the promise that she would come by in the morning that held them at bay. That, and the fact she told them they'd never get into the building. She wanted her family's support, but she needed this more.

"You can't possibly have enough energy to continue on this. And you'll over-tweak it."

Standing, she set a hand at her waist and leaned back over it. Her spine cracked and muscles stretched. She really wasn't tired after all. In fact, she was strung pretty tight, her brain racing to avoid thinking about Logan. "I'll polish it, and I want to go through our contacts until I find the right model. And someone who'll do the costumes."

"You're going to crash here, in case someone

could be at your home—"

"Nope. I was supposed to go to my sister's last night." She didn't say it was for an intervention, happy to have cut Jon off before he said the name that would never again be mentioned. "I canceled because we were rolling on this, so I'll head there for breakfast. They eat early because of the kids, and I'll be finished here and over to big sister's house before you roll out of bed to meet up with your tennis pro."

With a shrug, Jon shoved up and flexed his slender body. "I'm going. I'm of no further use to you."

"See you Monday."

Anticipating his intention to hug her again, Victoria slipped around the huge table and began to gather up the detritus of their meals and copious numbers of coffee cups. Jon hesitated, looking uncharacteristically awkward, before moving toward the door. "When do you want to schedule the shoot?"

"The sooner the better. We have a ton of other spreads in the wings, and putting this out front is going to cost us some timelines." Not that she regretted it, if he didn't.

Jon muttered something about costing *someone* in other ways and then gave her his trademark smile, the one that made all his staff give *him* their all. "It's well worth putting out ahead of our other projects, Tori. It's your heart and soul, and I hope it helps."

She winked and he laughed, though the worried look remained etched around his eyes. The project had helped, and it would continue to help. It was as though she'd parceled up so much of her angst and given it to someone else. "Have a great breakfast, Jon. And good luck with … afterward…"

"From your lips…"

As soon as the door clicked shut behind him, she

rifled through the files. Most of the models' information and headshots were on the company's server of course, but she wanted to *feel* the shots, hold the prints up in any and all positions until she found the perfect bone structure and form to suit her vision. She located the right woman after pulling five folders, and knew it, but diligently perused the rest until she'd examined them all before returning to number five. Alexia Dubrovka.

Thin and frail looking, although the model's appearance was misleading—they had to be tough as nails to stay fit and skinny and keep up with their profession. Huge, doe-like eyes framed with dark lashes stared out of a finely boned face. Gray, as she'd envisioned, almost silver. The high cheekbones, narrow nose and almost too-large lips on a slender face were the epitome of what Victoria held in her mind's eye.

Those lips would be emphasized, the cheekbones made out to be twin slashes, and the eyes... She closed her own and imagined the luminous tears that would glimmer and then fall to track down the pale cheeks. Perfect.

She'd insist on the blonde hair being partially upswept and held in place with a battered tiara beneath the ripped veil, while the rest would trail in tangled and defeated strands over the shoulders. And the gown... The layout boards spoke for themselves. Strategic rents and subtle yellowing in the folds would speak volumes to the camera and the observing eye. A heavy dress, to weigh the bride down further. The flowers were evocative, falling petals and a few blackened blood-red roses with their edges curled up, and thorns to mock the happy occasion. She'd sketched the perfect drop of blood on the model's fingertip.

With a shudder, she pulled herself from the vision and made several quick notes, posting them across the numerous drafts she and Jon had compiled. Perfect. Gathering up the chosen file, she made note of the contact information and fired off an email to the woman's agent. Fashion never slept, after all. She couched the request in casual terms, not wanting to sound too desperate, despite the hour, though six-ish wasn't an abnormal time for a person to be at work, even on a Sunday. She required complete autonomy over this spread, and the model was the medium and nothing else. The agent was one who liked to put his own spin on things, ingratiating himself, and she'd lose the model rather than suffer his input.

Stacking the rest of the files back into the cabinet, she took a quick look around before picking up her purse and phone. She'd stop in the ladies' to freshen up and then make her way to Juliana's for a calorie-busting breakfast and lose herself in the embrace of her family. She felt strangely hollow, but that was likely hunger.

Paige and Robert's car was pulled up behind her mom's in the driveway, and Victoria parked on the street. The only sounds were the birds scavenging the lawns for their breakfast and the occasional bark of a dog. Her shoes clattered along the sidewalk and she stepped around a bike dropped carelessly to sprawl across the concrete and adjoining grass.

This was the life she'd envisioned with Logan a few short years down the road, a house and kids in the suburbs, and her throat ached, closing against the loss. Calling up her courage, she pretended to smile despite her mouth's refusal to cooperate. It stood to reason that these types of things would remind her, at least for the next while. There was no way around it.

A flicker of anxiety flirted along the edges of her belly, silly because her family wouldn't expect anything more than she could offer. They knew her and how she coped. She ran up the steps, fatigue unexpectedly gnawing at her heels, and rapped on the door before entering.

"Tori!" Paige rushed her and wrapped her up. Victoria allowed herself a moment to revel in the warmth of her sister's arms, soaking in the familiar scent of jasmine, before stepping back.

"Hey, Paige. I can hear the urchins."

Brown eyes, for Paige had inherited her mom's coloring, studied her intently before her sister smiled. "They're helping Gramma make pancakes. The guys are grilling sausages and bacon outside and probably having a beer. Even if it's damn early. It's chaos. I'm glad you came, because we missed you last night."

Easing around Paige, Victoria headed to the kitchen from where happy food smells and joyful kid sounds emanated. "Probably for the best, sis. I expect you dissected the debacle. Saved me suffering through it, so I thank you."

"You've put it away like mom said. How do you do that?"

It was on the tip of her tongue to remind Paige that while she'd also suffered the loss of their father, she and Juliana had had him for years before Victoria came along. And that he'd treated them like princesses and her as the interloper. As someone never, ever enough. Like a plague—or a leper. So she'd had ample practice at denial. She halted and stared at Paige, feeling lightheaded.

"What's wrong?" Her sister moved in and grabbed her arm.

"I'm sorry Daddy left on my account, Paige. Well, mine and Mom's."

The faint color in Paige's face drained visibly, leaving her pale and drawn. "What are you talking about? Are you inferring that Dad left because of something you did?"

"No. Because of who I am. Or what I'm not."

"You're crazy. That fucking Logan."

Worn out, Victoria leaned against the wall and tried to focus on her sister's face. "That's a name I hope never to hear again."

"She's not crazy, just deluded." Juliana spoke quietly to Paige, having come down the hallway without either of them hearing her. "Tori, our father left because he's a sexist asshole who wanted a son to raise in his image because of some kind of whacked mid-life crisis. And accused Mom of failing him in the process. He didn't much care to hear that it's the man who determines the sex of the child because it didn't fit into his way of seeing things. I thought we'd settled this. Years ago."

"It's that other asshole's doing. He triggered this." Paige's pretty face was twisted with rage. "You were getting better."

Victoria flinched at the truth as she struggled to escape the grip of the past. "I'm sorry. I don't know why I said that out loud."

Juliana stroked her forearm. "You're feeling loss pretty keenly, I expect, and if you're as tired as you look, you aren't capable of processing intelligently. C'mon, we'll get you some food and maybe you'll consider there's nothing wrong with you. That the two important men in your life didn't leave because of you. It's all on them."

Maybe she *was* crazy—or deluded. Juliana had summed things up pretty succinctly. She said close to the same thing the shrink had spoken all those years ago, while warning Victoria to expect her father's abdication to impact her future relationships unless she guarded against it. Her mother said it too, though parsing it a little differently, probably because she'd borne much of the brunt. But, deep down, Victoria knew the truth. Logan had called off the wedding because of her ... her lack, so all the psychoanalyzing meant squat.

Her mother kissed her cheek and watched her with a tense expression, her lips tight and her smile not reaching her eyes, before the kids swarmed over, screaming her name and demanding she sit beside them. Both her sisters had put off having children until they were well established in their careers, so her nieces and nephews were all under the age of six. She didn't think there were better loved kids in the world. Certainly there were none sweeter or smarter.

"Auntie needs a coffee! You can take turns sitting with me. We can set the timer." She'd learned a thing or two about parenting from watching her sisters.

She sat down to an enormous cup of coffee and doused it with cream and a touch of raw sugar, the lattes but a fond memory. Murphy was in his highchair beside her and Patricia crowded her other elbow. The other kids pouted but agreed to her terms, although Sabrina glared at her cousins.

"Where's Unca Logan?" Mikey asked.

The adults froze for a moment before Victoria answered. "He's working, Pooh bear."

"I like him. He's funny."

"Of course you do." Paige offered him his choice of syrup and he was distracted.

It wasn't only her who would miss him, and her pain lurched to the surface. Finally, she got her breathing under control. Her mom went back to stacking pancakes at the stove. The patio doors slid open and Robert stuck his head in.

"You're here! Great. The meat's ready." A kind,

pleasant-looking guy, no one would ever see him as a high powered attorney, especially in khakis and a checkered shirt. She supposed lots of opponents underestimated his razor-sharp brain. He gave her a warm smile and his eyes said it all. A *great* guy. She was so happy for Paige, who was a force in her own right as a banker.

Michael pushed past, bearing a tray heaped high with fragrant bacon and sausage, and dumped it on the table, smack in the middle. Tall and lean, he was also one of the best real estate agents in the city, and he and Juliana made a formidable team. He gave her a warm and understanding smile.

The next hour was a feast, at least in the case of the rest of the bunch. Victoria pushed the food around her plate and listened to the casual conversation, punctuated by reminders from Mikey and Sabrina that it was their turn to sit with her. The elephant in the room huddled in the corner, away from little ears, but Victoria figured that would change as soon as the children went out to play.

The dishes stacked in the dishwasher, the leftover food packed away, and the table and countertops scrubbed, the adults settled back with more coffee. Michael pulled a couple of bottles from over the fridge and tipped a couple of ounces into proffered cups. She accepted the brandy gratefully, knowing she needed sleep sooner than later.

"Do you want to talk about it?" The lawyer took the floor and Victoria was most grateful. Cut and dried, black and white. Just what she needed.

"No."

"He set her back a couple of decades." Paige couldn't let it go.

"I won't slip again," she promised. "I've been up

all night working and like Juli said, I'm tired and not thinking straight."

"And he didn't say why." Robert put things back on track.

"He didn't."

"And she doesn't want to know." Her mom offered that tidbit.

Juliana fixed her husband with a glare. "Why would a man leave a woman at the altar?"

Michael shrugged. "Cold feet. He doesn't love her any more or not like he thought." The glance he shot his wife belied everything he'd said, but the latter was close enough to Victoria's truth that it lanced deep. "I just don't see it in this case."

She hurried to interrupt and ignored the pain. "Does it matter?" she asked, as she looked around the table. "It's done. Trust is everything in a relationship."

Everyone nodded somberly, and silence reigned, because how could anyone challenge that fact?

"I can't stand to be pitied by my family. I need to move on, better than languishing. Please."

All gazes blinked away from her, some to scan outside where the kids were, others to stare elsewhere. When her family members looked her way again, she saw nothing but love and acceptance.

"Thanks. I'll be fine."

What choice did she have? Well, she could fall apart like she did as a child when her dad left, before she found succor in schooling, or she could be an adult. There might come a time when she'd allow herself to get in touch with her old shattered self, but it was something she couldn't allow right now if she was to survive.

"Whatever you need." Juliana spoke quietly and was echoed by everyone else. Her mom blinked tears away and worked her fingers through Victoria's,

45

squeezing tight.

A creaking yawn broke the tension, and Paige chuckled. "Why don't you say goodbye to the kids and have a sleep. Juliana made the spare room up for you."

"I'll do that."

****

Her phone chimed and woke her. She wasn't certain where she was for a moment and then recognized the picture mounted on the far wall. The house was essentially silent with the exception of the whirr of the air conditioning. Being a Sunday, they'd probably taken the children someplace to enjoy the sunny day before the work week started.

She'd expected to find sleep difficult, but the exhausting events and the all-nighter had obviously drained her reserves—and probably the brandy hadn't hurt. After falling into bed, slumber had tugged her deep. Oh, she'd dreamed a little, fragments of them stuck to her subconscious to rasp like sandpaper.

Logan wouldn't leave her alone, even in sleep, and she absently scrubbed at the residual salty tracks on her cheeks. Stretching, she forced the rush of memory back—this should have been day one of the first full day of married life—and instead selected a recollection she could deal with. Work. Yes, work had gone well yesterday, and she could foresee great things coming out of it.

The chime was an email notification, and she fumbled her phone from the nightstand. The blinds were drawn, but enough daylight, compliments of the bright sunshine, filtered in, and she searched the small screen.

The agent for Alexia the model had replied and invited a contract. That meant a trip back to the office, but she had nothing better to do with her time, so she climbed out of bed. Wearing the t-shirt Juliana had loaned her, and her panties, she listened at the door to ensure everyone was out and pattered down the hall to the bathroom.

A shower and a light application of makeup later, she helped herself to her sister's closet and pulled the clean clothes on. Stuffing hers into a bag, she wrote a note of explanation and locked up. Having a pressing project lifted her spirits and kept her focus away from yesterday—it felt like years had passed, so what was that simmering hurt so near the surface?

Was she a coward? Maybe if she knew exactly why Logan had rejected her, she could guard against it with others... Her teeth ground furiously. She wasn't going to go there. She'd as much as promised her family she wouldn't blame herself, so she had to let the old Victoria go. And nothing was going to interfere with her work. She also never planned to open herself up to another man, ever, so why bother to consider it? *Curiosity killed the cat, satisfaction drew it back.* She quashed the stupid quote flat in her head.

Paying attention to her driving and the rest of the drivers on the road, she pulled up to the office building. It was like an oasis, a place of safety, and the awfulness that had created the need for such a thing nearly choked her. But better this place than none, because she didn't think her little house would be a sanctuary, not when she'd see Logan at every turn. And he still had a key... If she was so goddamn fine, why was the pain leaking through?

Electing to park at a meter, she clambered out of the car, and made her way to the door. She wondered if Jon would object to a cot being set up someplace, maybe in one of the storage areas. She could shower at the gym and... Okay, so work was going to be her life from here on in. That didn't mean she was going to live here, for

God's sake, though the idea eased the roiling in her gut.

Gaining her office, she accessed the contracts and drafted one for her chosen model and then called Jon.

"Tori? What's wrong?"

"Nothing. I'm sorry to interrupt." What was she thinking? It was Sunday!

"We're heading back to my place. What do you need?" Her boss sounded a little tense.

"Maybe it can wait until tomorrow."

"What do you need, sweetie?"

She explained her contact with the agent, texting Jon a headshot of the model. He approved, giving her a sense of relief. She hadn't forged ahead without consultation like this in the past and was regretting it now. Fortunately, Jon seemed to understand.

He also accepted the terms of the draft contract. "Send it off. But we'll deal with any changes tomorrow."

"Okay."

"Now, take the rest of the day off, Tori. Seriously. I'll see you tomorrow."

After dealing with the contract, she had nothing else to do and the evening loomed large. She crept into the design room to view the mock ups—and wept.

****

Logan couldn't remember a time he'd been so tired. Victoria had dropped out of sight, her family insisting she wasn't around. They treated him with icy disdain, tinted with curiosity, and he was glad he wasn't face-to-face with her brothers-in-law. Although her sisters would probably do more damage when he thought about it.

It had been a calculated risk to call the people he had in an attempt to reach her, but none of them would give his father the time of day. Hell, they hadn't given him any.

It occurred that he might consult with Robert Vermette. A lawyer distant from the company would be an excellent choice, especially one with the skills to represent him as fiercely as would be required. And the man wouldn't breach confidentiality so his father would never know. He wasn't above building a bridge to Victoria's family for later, either.

He'd waited for her in her little house late into the night, falling asleep on the couch and waking with a crick in his neck. Where had she stayed? Maybe she'd left town. Part of him was relieved not to face her, because he couldn't yet tell her why he'd done what he had. But he had to see her, needed to assure himself she was all right. Beg her to give him some time. His mother assured him Victoria's mom would let her know if things were dire, but he had to see for himself.

He'd made good initial progress in unraveling the web his father had spun, but it was tedious, and he had a long way to go. He supposed taking it apart was easier than putting it together, but the old man had months to scheme and get things in place. And Logan had been too distracted by his lovely fiancée to notice. His body hardened, merely thinking about her. They hadn't spent this much time apart in months, and he was starving for her. His bright, beautiful Victoria, so fragile at times behind her confident persona.

His chest squeezed, knowing how badly he'd hurt her. Without asking, he knew he'd confirmed that deep-seated fear that she held—that she wasn't enough for him. Because of what her father had imprinted in her. In truth, *he* wasn't good enough for *her* and had been terrified she'd figure it out before he tied her to him with a wedding ring and hopefully a child or several. The old man had landed a terrible strike, and it remained to be seen if it was the deathblow. Logan didn't think he could go on if that was the case.

Knowing he had to slip away, he'd penned a brief note, the contents reflecting each and every text and voice mail he'd left her. *Give me some time. Then I can explain. I love you. L*

Folding it, he scribbled her name on the front in huge letters and stuck it to the fridge with a magnet. He'd never given up on anything worthwhile in his life, and wasn't going to start with the woman of his dreams.

Chapter Three

"What did you do?" Jon's handsome face wore a look of horror.

"What? You don't like it?" Victoria lifted a hand to her head and tentatively brushed it over the short strands there. "I thought I looked classy."

His features smoothing out, her boss said, "You do. You're classically beautiful and you'd look wonderful bald, wearing burlap. But your lovely hair…"

"Braided it, hacked it off and donated it to a salon that makes wigs for people undergoing chemo. I can always grow it back."

"True. I guess it's just because I envied you that mane of yours."

"You're such a girl, sometimes."

"True." He narrowed his eyes. "Are you putting anything in that body of yours other than coffee?"

Saluting him with her cup, she brushed past into the office. Nothing else appealed, and actually, the thought of food made her feel ill. "I switched to half-caf."

"Not what I asked."

"Quit fretting, Jon. I'm good."

"Where are you staying?"

"At Juliana's, just for a couple of nights. Why?"

He sighed. "The one I shall not name has called several times. Apparently, you haven't been home."

Her gut clenched. She'd been in and out to change out her clothes and pick up a few things. Logan had been in her house. His familiar scent was too recent to miss, which was why she wasn't sleeping there. "I don't much feel like staying at home," she admitted.

"Well, you aren't going to live here. And don't tell me you haven't thought about it."

"I have. But I won't if you say so."

Jon shoved the door closed, knowing as well as she did that their secretary could spread gossip faster than butter on hot toast. "Tori, you've been working harder than me. Well, longer hours. That's scary. I'm worried about you."

"What for? I'm fine."

"It's like the ... wedding fiasco never happened. Because you're sublimating it with work."

"Fancy word," she teased. "And if I am? What else would you have me do? Mope? Eat gallons of ice cream? Drink? Work is my drug of choice."

"I guess I can't argue with that."

"But?"

"It's not the best choice. Maybe you could talk to someone, like a professional."

She sighed. "Jon, let it go. Please."

"I'll try. But Tori, Logan would really like to talk with you."

Her hand tightened around her latte. "So my mother says, and Robert, too, for some unknown reason—or at least one he can't disclose. And now you. I was hoping for a little loyalty, Jon."

"You have mine, sweetie. Know that. But I want what's best for you."

"And you think the man who *jilted* me right at the freaking altar is best for me?"

"There might be a good explanation."

Her boss, her good friend couldn't see what was right in front of his face, but then theirs was a different relationship. She'd work herself to the bone for him and never let him down. That's what he expected and what she was capable of giving. A friendship was there, as well, but not the kind of intimacy… "Jon. I'm not sure why he's calling, but anything that needs saying can be couriered. I'll sign off on anything necessary."

"I don't think that's what it's about."

"It doesn't matter."

"Are you absolutely sure?"

She somehow set her coffee down and folded her hands together to control the trembling. People had to quit talking to her about him. She'd ducked Kate's calls, and Theresa's for this very reason. Hurting other people because she couldn't do this.

With exaggerated calm, she said, "Certain. I'm not stupid, Jon, nor a masochist. If I keep him far away, he can't hurt me again. That's really important to me, because I don't think…" His stricken face told her he understood that she couldn't come back a second time. Third, in truth, but who was counting?

"Got it. Then sit down, because I have a proposition for you."

Dropping into a client chair, she picked up her cup again. "Something good?"

"I opened a branch of the company on the east coast last year as you know, and my CEO just resigned. I need someone out there to spearhead the campaigns."

"Me? I'm not qualified."

"Not on paper. But you have a lot of experience. You've also worked in most every department here, or overseen projects, and you know me. What I expect."

Leave California? Leave her family? Leave … Logan? "For how long?"

"Minimum six months but possibly up to a year. And if I don't find someone and you like it, then for however long."

"If I can do it. Well."

"That goes without saying. You might be my best

employee and my dear friend, but—"

"Business is business and love is bullshit. I know." She'd heard it often enough, although Jon had a soft core he tried hard not to show.

"Take a couple of days—"

"No need. I can be on the next plane." Her family would take care of her house, rent it out, whatever.

"Now I know you're a freaking mess." Jon crossed to the window and peered out, obviously wanting to say more.

Speaking to his back, she said, "How could I not be, my friend? Seriously? This opportunity will give me the distance I need and the time to put myself back together or at least rebuild. I'll be too busy to fret."

"You won't have any support," he warned. "Your family's here."

"The magic of the telephone, Jon. And my mother loves to fly."

"I'll get Myrna to make the arrangements for tomorrow. Give you time to pack and whatever. The company has a small apartment there, fully furnished. Any visiting executives will have to use a hotel because it's yours."

"Hugs. Now let's talk about Tattered Bride." They had reserved space in a variety of small presses as well as Jon's own E-zine for the anticipated sales, and the shoot would soon be underway.

"Transfer it to Boston."

"Really?

"It's your conception. See it through to the end. Just make the deadline."

"Done."

She spent a little time packing a small box up from her desk, though avoided the rest of the staff. Except for Myrna. She found the woman in the break room, staring into the fridge.

"Myrna."

Her secretary jumped. "Oh, hey. Sorry. Looking for my yogurt, but it's gone. I swear I'm gonna put a nanny cam in here. And when I find out who is taking my food…"

"Have you made my flight arrangements yet?"

"Sure. I emailed them to you. For tomorrow, right?" Myrna plucked an apple from the shelf. "I wonder how long this has been in there?"

"Tomorrow," Victoria agreed, ignoring the fruit question. "I'm going to ask something of you."

About to take a bite, the other woman obviously heard the seriousness in her tone. "Okay."

"If people call here for me, I want you to say I'm no longer working here. And that's it. Refer them to Jon."

Myrna wrinkled her brow. "Not that you've been transferred to Boston?"

"Not that you know where I am, period. You don't have to lie. Simply say that I'm no longer here and you're not at liberty to give out additional information. Jon will deal with them."

Understanding washed over Myrna's face. "Oh, right. I get it. A fresh start after … everything."

"Exactly. Thanks. And Myrna? News of my new position will get out soon enough, but no one but you and I, and Jon know for now." Victoria watched her secretary's eyes and knew the message had been received.

"You can count on me to keep it quiet."

Returning to her office, she tucked the box under her arm and poked her head in to say goodbye to Jon. "No gushy stuff. But thanks again. I'll read the files on the plane. And Jon? I won't let you down."

"I know you won't." He got up and came to hug her. "Gushy stuff isn't bad between friends, sweetie. I want Facetime every evening, and you call if you need to."

Squeezing him tight, she blinked back tears. If she started that nonsense she'd cry forever. "I will. Be good. Or not."

"Get gone. See your family and break the news. Pack. Whatever. It'll be strange around here without you."

She took the stairs, instead of the elevator and was puffing by the time she reached the street. Much of her clothing was already packed, in preparation for moving into Logan's condo, so she hauled those cases out to her vehicle. It didn't take long to gather up the rest of the items she thought she might need, although there was nothing for a Boston winter. Well, that's what shopping was about. She added a few keepsakes and some pictures to make her new place feel homey.

There wasn't much in the fridge, because she was supposed to have moved out, so she emptied the rest into the garbage, and then turned it off, propping open the doors. Her name jumped out at her and she reached a shaking hand out to touch the note.

Freeing it from the magnet, she held it carefully, as one might hold a sleeping snake. If she read it, what would it do to her plans? Would whatever he'd written cause her to leave herself open for additional pain? Curiosity dulled as she considered her options. Better she left well enough alone, like deleting those spam messages that promised such wonderful things if only one would click on the link... She *knew* better.

Crumpling the paper, she dropped it on top of the odds and ends from the refrigerator, and managed to leave it there, though the corners curled up to give a tantalizing glimpse of Logan's handwriting. As she shut down the hot water tank, the enormity of what she was undertaking rolled over her. She sank onto a kitchen chair and rubbed her forehead. She'd made the commitment, and she kept her promises, but was she overreacting? Was this opportunity actually flight? Her family was going to ask the same questions, and she didn't want to wing it.

Wrapping her arms around her ribs in an awkward parody of a hug, she whimpered, a loud sound in the quiet space without even the humming of the fridge to offset it. She missed Logan. She missed everything about him, from the way he made her laugh, to feeling confident and special … his handsome face, brilliant mind, and innate kindness. She longed for him beside her at night, both recovering from strenuous lovemaking that cemented their bond.

Sometimes he would turn to her in the dark, and she'd be ready for him with a mere touch, ready for him to slip inside of her. No one made her feel the way he did. And that was what made his rejection all the more agonizing.

A scalding sob tore up her throat, choking her and making her gasp. How did good men hide their darkness so that the women who loved them didn't see? Or was she blind, blinded by how deeply in love she'd been? There had been no sign, nothing. Had there? She knew a braver woman would face Logan, now he had something to say, and read that note. But she couldn't bring herself to hear it. Fool me once… She'd wither up and blow away a second time, the husk that would be left, and she owed herself—and her family—more than that. Trust was everything.

Using a dishtowel to dry her face, she admonished herself. It was time to move on. People did it all the time, and she wasn't special, no different. She'd either lie down, giving in, or she'd pick herself up and carry on. With the pep talk complete, she stuffed the towel in the garbage and hauled it and the last case outside, snapping off the light and locking up. Done.

She made the drive to her sister's on autopilot, and took three tries to park close enough to the curb, before making her way inside. The usual cacophony of sound greeted her and she swept both kids into her arms and settled them on either hip.

"Your face is puffed." Her niece patted her cheek. "Like Topsy."

Topsy being Sabrina's dumpling of a doll, Victoria winced. "I have the sniffles."

Mikey tweaked her nose. "Sniffles."

"Right." She smiled widely. "C'mon, you two. Your dad probably made a great dinner."

"Macaroni," they both crowed and she squeezed them tight. She'd miss the kids so much.

"You couldn't have picked someplace further to run to? Like New Zealand?" Juliana made coffee after putting the kids to bed. Dinner had been a quiet affair, thanks to macaroni and cheese, and Victoria had gotten away with one bedtime story each. "What'd Mom say?" her sister continued.

"She's on her way. I called her. She and Frank are at dinner, but she'll be along. Paige can't bring the kids, so I'll see her in the morning before I leave. Robert's coming over, though." She frowned. "Maybe he thinks I need legal advice."

Michael slammed the door on the dishwasher. "You have a place to live there? Because I have contacts."

"I'm good. I'll stay in the company apartment. If I end up living in Boston, I'll be asking for advice on the best area to live in, though."

"You aren't staying there. Not forever." Juli dumped containers of sugar and cream on the table. "This is an adventure. A challenging career move to keep you so busy you won't fall apart and a way to heal, right? Your way of healing."

"Exactly."

"So it's not forever."

There was no forever. "Don't get excited, Juli. It was a comment. That's all." Except she wasn't going to want to see Logan with his next woman, ever, and while the city was big, it was inevitable she'd run into him. Them. If she lived here. She parted her lips to take in a cleansing breath without making it obvious.

"Sure." Her sister poured coffee and sat across from her, badgering her with questions about the new job, without another reference to Logan. Bless her.

Her mother arrived shortly, at the same time as Robert, and wasn't as freaked as Victoria expected.

"I'll miss you, one of my girls so far away, Tori, but if you're determined to leave Logan behind, it might be for the best."

Leave Logan behind? He'd jilted *her*, for God's sake. "Mom? Logan left me, remember?"

"And he's reaching out. Maybe it's to make amends. Men get cold feet. Things happen."

"They do," Robert intoned, looking very lawyerly. Except for a swollen right hand, the knuckle in the middle a dark purple.

"What?" She stared at her brother-in-law. "What's going on? And what happened to your hand?"

He shrugged and tucked it in his pocket. "I jammed it in something. And I was merely agreeing with your mother. Paige would rather you stay here."

"And you came over to tell me that? I'm seeing

her tomorrow."

Maybe he didn't have the perfect lawyer face because she saw a flicker of wariness. "Robert."

He lifted a shoulder. "I think you could be making a mistake, Victoria. Leaving. Call it lawyer's intuition."

"Is there something about the paperwork I signed? With Logan?" There was no pre-nup. He'd refused, even though his father had strongly recommended it. To avoid alienating the older man, she'd insisted on signing an agreement that bound her to give up any and all interests in the Doherty Holdings, in the event of a divorce. Robert had reviewed it.

"I checked," he admitted. "Just to be sure. It's good."

"Did my mother say something about suing?" She bent a suspicious stare on her parent.

"No! Only to you," her mom replied.

"Well, then it seems there's no reason to stay." She knew her mother wouldn't have taken her father back. She didn't think... "You're all welcome to visit. Right?"

There was a chorus of agreement, and if reluctant, so be it.

"And there's no need for anyone to know where I've gone, okay? At least not at first. I mean, our family and close friends should know, but not... I just need some time. And I don't want to be fielding any contact without you there to support me."

Her family members all promised, accepting what she didn't say.

"The kids are going to be so upset to lose their favorite Auntie," Juli said. "They grow so fast."

"Come see me. Take a holiday." She'd miss them terribly, and a year was a long time in kidlet years. But she needed to do this for herself.

"Will you deal with my house, Mom? Rent it or whatever?"

"Juli and I will take care of it, Tori." Michael eased her mind. "I have likely tenants."

"I'll take you to the airport in your car. I can park it at my house until you come home." Her mother always planned ahead, having been forced to learn how, when her husband left. Victoria shivered at the comparison.

"Thanks, Mom. And you will come visit? Soon? You and Frank? I'll send plane tickets."

"Of course."

The remainder of the evening passed with discussions about Boston and whether a trip to New York was plausible, considering the workload ahead of her. Victoria basked in one last time with her family for the foreseeable future, though Paige and the kids would fill her morning. Logan had fit in so well here, and she suffered a pang of remorse when she again considered that everyone else was grieving his loss as well. It just didn't pay to let someone in, and she fiercely prayed that her sisters' husbands remained tried and true. Paige and Juliana weren't like her, though, so the chances were good.

****

He let himself into her little house, a bit surprised she hadn't changed the locks, but why would she when she obviously wasn't sleeping here? Walking through the living room, one of the coziest spaces he'd ever been inside, he thought he noticed some things missing. His pace picked up, and he checked the bedroom. Her cases were gone, the ones he'd seen her pack when she was organizing for the move to his condo.

It had been difficult for her to agree to give up the place she'd worked hard to purchase and then fixed up so carefully. But his condo was larger and more suitable for them as a couple. Logan Doherty and his wife. Because that's how it must have seemed, though Victoria had gracefully given in. Just as she'd signed off on any interest in the business. That alone should have eased his old man, but instead, he despised her weakness. A weakness for him, Logan, who she sacrificed for so willingly.

The fridge had been emptied and he had to accept his Victoria had moved out. But to where? He'd seen her car at her oldest sister's—stalking wasn't something he'd envisioned for himself, but it had meant she was safe, with family. His note was gone... Yet she hadn't called him. So she couldn't even grant him some time, she was so hurt.

Pulling his cell out, he punched in a number. "Margaret? It's Logan again." He could hear several voices in the background, and strained to hear if one of them was Victoria's. So many people called her Tori, but her full name was so beautiful. So like her.

In a hushed voice, Margaret said, "Logan, I've asked her to talk with you. She won't. It's very final. You have to understand... Hell, *I* don't understand."

"I'll tell you why as soon as I can. I'll tell you all. I promise. But I want to offer Victoria a confidential promise. That what happened wasn't because of her—or me—it was beyond my control." It *was* because of her, if only in his father's twisted way of thinking, but that didn't count. And he sure as hell wasn't telling her mother that. "I've asked her for more time. Tell her that I love her."

"She doesn't trust you anymore, Logan. That's a huge thing. And she refuses to give you another opportunity to hurt her. My Tori learned her lesson well, and nothing any of us say changes it. I'm sorry. Because

I believe you. I don't know why, other than I saw how much you loved my daughter."

"I *love* her, Margaret. Not past tense. Not ever past tense. Where did she go?"

Silence. He counted the seconds before she responded, "You know?"

"I'm at her house. She took her things, cleaned out the fridge."

"I can't tell you. I promised. We all promised."

So Robert couldn't tell him either, despite agreeing to represent him earlier today. Reluctantly agreeing to honor client-attorney privilege after Logan jammed a dollar in his pocket and pronounced him hired for fifteen minutes. The financial insult might have provoked the punch in the mouth, though he suspected Robert had really hit him because of what he'd done to Victoria.

The lawyer was on board now, however, his curiosity piqued to the extent of hearing Logan out. He was horrified at the old man's perfidy and promised to do what he could, but his loyalties would have been torn… And he was bound by ethics too.

"I'll find her. And when I do, it'll be time to tell her." He gingerly touched his split lip, welcoming the pain.

"You will, I'm sure. But I fear it's too late."

Her words, delivered in such a fatalistic tone, scared the shit out of him. She knew her child, better than him, and what he knew told him she could be right. The Victoria he knew would have responded to his note, to any of his desperate communications. He'd destroyed a piece of his woman, and she might not recognize him anymore. He might not know *her*.

Chapter Four

Logan's mouth sealed over hers with a perfect fit, his tongue licking along the seam of her lips to slide between them in a possessive movement that mimicked the way his cock stretched the walls of her channel. She arched into his solid body, seeking that thick hardness between her thighs.

Instead, he tore his lips away to kiss along the curve of her jaw and then down the length of her throat, pausing to suck at the sweet spot where her neck met her shoulder. Victoria whimpered with pleasure and ran her hands over the firm flesh of his back. Muscles moved smoothly beneath her questing touch, the heat of him drawing her closer.

He didn't murmur his usual endearments or the sexy, filthy comments about how he loved her body, especially her lady parts, instead moving lower to pay homage to her breasts. He plumped them with his big hands, offering them up to his talented mouth. Lashing each beaded tip with his tongue, he teased and tormented until she whined for more. For his cock inside of her. "Please. Please, Logan."

Teasing her with a fingertip, he trailed along her swollen labia, dancing inside the slippery folds to circle her entrance. Her clit ached for his touch and her legs fell open to accommodate him as he found the tiny nub. He drew moisture along to anoint it and slipped back the protective hood. Faster, he worked it, rubbing in tiny circles and her orgasm built. She needed him to fill her. She needed...

Victoria woke, one hand clasping her breast, the other buried between her thighs, on the cusp of a momentous climax. She yanked her hands away from her body and fisted them as her heart raced and the blood pounded in her temples. Struggling to sit, she wheezed in despair, the sound of her breath rattling in the small bedroom.

She stood, wavering until she gained her balance and made her way to the bathroom. A splash of cold water woke her fully, and she accepted she was in Boston, in the company's furnished apartment, alone. No Logan.

Shivering, she peered at her reflection in the harsh light over the vanity mirror. Her sleep shirt was rumpled, falling loosely over a long, thin body barely maintained by caffeine and the occasional protein bar consumed at her desk. And let's not forget the banana she nibbled at the insistence of her new secretary, Dawna.

The hollows beneath her cheekbones weren't as sexy as the ones the model for The Tattered Bride sported, but she wasn't going for that look anyhow. Especially with the dark circles under her eyes. Grimacing, she ran her fingers through her cropped hair and left the strands in spiked disarray. The starving, waif characteristics really weren't her and she needed to do something about that. Soon.

With a sigh, she turned away, having distracted herself enough to forget about her erotic dream. If she let herself think about how Logan invaded her sleep, it was only because she was grateful she could banish thoughts of him during the fourteen- and sixteen-hour days she was working.

There was no point in returning to bed. Six o'clock was just around the corner, and she should make coffee. She set the pot to drip. Though she had a single-serve machine in her office, she liked the lure of a full carafe while she readied for the day. Victoria headed back to the bathroom to shower and spend the ever-increasing minutes to repair the ravages exhaustion and bone-deep despair wrought on her face. Like a bad stretch of weather, a drought, it had to break soon.

Her fingers strayed to her apex where her clit still begged for attention, and in a few minutes she drew out a small, indifferent orgasm. The mechanics of bringing herself off were familiar, but only because she kept waking from those dreams, her body aching with unrequited passion and need.

She stood, bowed beneath the spray of water and summoned the energy to get to the office. It was Saturday—no, Sunday—but she'd get ahead of next week's schedule and inspire the rest of the staff to perform their utmost. Already they'd nicknamed her The Tireless Bitch, and she hoped it was spoken with affection, at least sometimes.

Part of her longed to crawl back into the double bed and lose herself in the oblivion of sleep, but even that was denied her. Damn him. She avoided any media that might update her as to his life, and her family and friends never mentioned him—at all. It hadn't been a long time, barely a month since that infamous day, okay, three weeks, six days and sixteen hours, ten minutes, give or take a few seconds, but it felt like yesterday when her defenses were down.

So don't let them drop, stupid. With a start, she listened to that impatient, inner voice and snapped the water off. Grabbing a towel, she wrapped herself up and rubbed the moisture from her hair with a smaller one.

Winter was around the corner, and she thought she might take a little time to find a suitable pair of boots and a coat, maybe a jacket, too, in preparation. Some warmer clothes for the office. The idea wasn't terribly palatable, but she didn't have a personal shopper. Though Dawna would be chewing at her heels soon if she didn't purchase some suitable apparel. The woman had elected herself Victoria's mother away from home, and worse, had forged some kind of alliance with her real mom.

A small smile etched her lips as she dug out her makeup. The staff in Boston were all pretty great, much like back in California, although she had to step on Jason a time or two. Once he'd accepted she wasn't fresh fodder for his man-whoring ways, he'd shown respect for her position.

Smoothing moisturizer over her skin, she sniffed to ensure the coffee was perking, satisfied by the aroma permeating the apartment. She hung up her towels and headed to pour a cup, belting a robe around her as she went.

A dollop of cream and a teaspoon of sugar in the biggest cup she'd found in the cupboard joined the dark brew and she inhaled before taking a sip. It occurred it was the only pleasure in her life, and she took a bigger gulp, burning her mouth.

"Ow." She startled herself and laughed. "Losing it, Tori. Fucking sad commentary on your life."

A sob caught her by surprise because she hadn't cried since moving here, the flight eaten up with reviewing the files Jon provided. The long days of work saw her fall into bed in utter exhaustion to sleep heavily—and dream.

"No." If she was going to talk to herself, it would be for the better. "You aren't going back to that." Back to missing Logan so badly she felt she could cry a river and still never release the pain.

Her determination was effective, because her angst crept back to crouch in the tiny cell she'd built, and the door slammed shut, the lock catching. If she didn't feed it or let it see the light of day, surely it would vanish, or at least be absorbed and cease to trouble her.

She dressed, in a fairly casual outfit in deference to it being a Sunday, again noting the need to ask Dawna for the name of a good tailor before her skirts fell down, and headed out. The weekend security guy yanked open the door for her.

"Morning, Mizz Sparrow. Going to work?"

"Always, Emilio. Just like you." She knew he worked two jobs to provide for his family, a wife and two little boys with another on the way.

"You work too hard. You have no ... social life!"

"Like you." She strode past him with a smile.

"But I had one before," he called after her.

Her confident steps faltered. Before. What was it about today? She had to quit thinking about the past and allowing things to remind her. She walked a few blocks, enjoying the crispness in the air that foretold the coming of fall, before flagging a cab.

The office was empty, as she expected. Jon was probably working back home, but maybe not. She'd spent an hour on Facetime with him yesterday, and he'd confided he and the tennis pro were becoming an item. Her boss in a committed relationship? She'd believe that when it really happened, like if he put a ring on it.

Pulling up the layout and schedule for The Tattered Bride, she gave the final approval. Unheard of, but under two weeks to publication across various venues. Jon had been correct. It was her baby, and she'd poured her grief and loss into the project, finding it to be a huge motivator. If only it had totally cleansed the way she'd hoped, instead of providing only that initial relief.

But model Alexia killed it, and several brands snapped the image up, Victoria's favorite being a woman's perfume with dark, sultry undernotes. The book-cover option ran out at the end of the month, but she had no doubt it too would be taken. Hopefully not by another vampire series, although a bloodless tattered bride wasn't so far off the mark when she thought about it.

Focusing her mind on all the other projects, one by one, she reviewed and made notes on them. The hours went by, and she absently chewed on a protein bar and sipped at another latte.

Her cell vibrated across the desktop, and she jerked her attention away from her work, noting the darkening of the day. "Hello?"

"Are you working on a Sunday?"

"Yes, Mom." It was great to hear her mother's voice, even the lecturing one.

"When do you take a day off?"

"I don't. I'm waiting for you to come visit so we can play tourist."

"That'll be tomorrow then."

Victoria squealed and covered her mouth, casting a glance around her office, regardless she was the only one in the building. "Really? When? What time?"

"I'll be there after lunch." Her mother rattled the flight number and details off. "Is it convenient?"

"Of course, it is! Just you, or—"

"Just me. Frank hates flying and your sisters are overwhelmed at work right now."

"I'll pick you up."

"Any chance you can take a few hours off?"

"More than a few, Mom. We're up to date here and everything is under control." In truth, more than under control. Her staff had days of work ahead of them as a result of her diligent efforts today, and a staff meeting tomorrow morning would confirm deadlines and clear up any questions. "We can go shopping too."

It was so good to hear her mother was coming, that Victoria decided to go grocery shopping to give the appearance of having food in her apartment. They'd eat out, do the tourist thing, but it would nice to offer her mother nourishment of some sort.

She closed down the office and took a cab to a twenty-four-hour market, filling a basket with things that might never get opened, but gave her a sense of accomplishment. Her hand on a ripe peach, she hesitated, drawing back as the memory of Logan peeling one for her, the sweet juices running down his hand as he tucked it between her lips… They'd both been naked, in his bed, sticky and—

With a shake of her head, she moved to the grapes and selected a bunch. It was getting easier to banish those memories, the ones that snuck up on her to infiltrate and wreak havoc on her equilibrium. If her hands shook a little and her belly clenched with arousal, it didn't last long.

Carrying the sacks into her apartment, she put everything away before changing into another sleep shirt. It seemed early to go to bed—and she'd be sure to dream about Logan and peaches—so she flicked on the television, reluctant to stream anything on her phone or laptop. It felt too much like work.

Curled up on the couch with a cup of herbal tea— perhaps minimizing her caffeine intake would mean no more dreams—she scrolled through the channels. She'd flicked past a news station when her brain caught up with what her eyes had telegraphed. Fumbling, she reversed the order but couldn't find it.

She set her cup down, the contents spilling over to scald her fingers, and she sucked two of them into her mouth, ignoring the pain as she headed for her laptop.

Calling up a search engine, she typed in the keywords and held her breath as the information came up, several listings in fact.

Clicking on the latest, she watched as pictures with captions filled the screen. Pictures of Logan, and his mother. A few of him with his siblings, and a few with people she had a vague recollection of. A separate one of his father. All of them recent. She reached a wavering hand toward Logan's image, touching one fingertip to his face. He looked drawn and fatigued, his face thin and his eyes sunken. She trembled, and couldn't swallow the saliva pooling in her mouth.

Scanning the information, she grasped the basics: Logan had led a business coup of sorts, rallying the board and shareholders to oust his father. His mother and siblings had backed him and the headlines read like something out of a military takeover. *Son ousts Patriarch! Long-time Businessman Stripped of Title! Prince beheads King!*

What had happened? She knew working for his father made Logan insane on many occasions, and the senior Doherty wasn't a nice man—to anyone. But he was powerful and wealthy. Very business savvy. Why had Logan done it? And how?

Scrolling, she read nothing that gave her further insight, only basic information about the takeover. There were more pictures of Logan, new captions titling him the New King of Doherty Holdings. Her finger paused on the pad, and a cold fist squeezed her insides. The elegant blonde standing at Logan's shoulder, the one with the adoring look on her striking features, appeared in nearly all the subsequent images. *Adrienne Parker.*

Knowing she was twisting the knife, she searched the woman's name and confirmed she had joined the Doherty firm three months prior to the wedding. The non-wedding. Logan had never mentioned her, despite Adrienne holding the position of his father's personal assistant. That in itself should tell anyone something. She was tired of speculating, of wondering, and it should be a relief to finally know. She hadn't been enough for Logan, but it stung like salt in an open wound that another woman had waited in the wings—or had been center stage.

There was some kind of a weird triangle operating and her imagination ran rampant. Sean Doherty was having an affair with this Adrienne and Logan wanted her. So he cleared the way by calling off the wedding and then had his father voted off the board, obtaining her for himself.

Sean hated Victoria so hired Adrienne to tempt Logan. It worked. He decided not to marry Victoria, then Sean decided he wanted Adrienne for himself. He and Logan faced off and Logan won. To the winner went the spoils.

Logan's womanizing history and his preference for big-titted blondes colored her take, she knew that. He hadn't looked at anyone else since the date they met if she believed him. And she did. Had. She dropped her face into her hands and tried to clear her head. She had no idea what to believe and wished she hadn't given into prurient curiosity.

Regardless, a huge change had taken place at Doherty Holdings, taking its toll on Logan, though his well-being was probably in good hands. Blonde hands. She reminded herself it didn't matter, because she was no longer remotely involved or interested. Erasing her browser history didn't change the fact she'd broken her rule of no updates, no cyber stalking, no displaying interest in one Logan Doherty. And now she couldn't decide if being replaced felt better than him finding her inadequate. Except it was the same thing.

She cleaned up the tea and set the cup in the sink, moving mechanically as she went through her bedtime routine. Her mother would arrive tomorrow—a welcome distraction—and the day after would take care of itself. She'd taken a step backward, but there was nothing she could do about it, except carry on. And on.

****

Logan wasn't sure if he had the wherewithal to go out to his car and make the drive home. The past few weeks had been filled with moments of inspiration but primarily gut-wrenching subterfuge. The press conference had been carefully orchestrated, the legalities perfected by none other than Robert Vermette and his firm, and the timing ... exquisite. His father had been at his country house for the weekend, and unavailable for comment—unable to mount a viable defense. Nothing like administering his own medicine to give Logan utter satisfaction.

Keeping up appearances in front of the old man had taken the bulk of his energy, but somehow he'd pulled it off. No word of his attempts to reach out to Victoria had leaked. His father actually patted him on the back on one occasion and congratulated him.

"You did the right thing, boy. She'd have been a millstone around your neck, what with no real connections. I hear she's moved away. Best thing for both of you. Time now to consider a woman who'll be a benefit to your future and that of the company."

Funny how he could recall only that side of the conversation, right down to the way the old man's lips twisted and his eyes gleamed. He must have responded appropriately, because his dad hadn't put his nefarious plan into action and was still walking around, breathing.

Dismantling the scheme had been an exercise in

extreme skill and caution. It helped that he'd found an ally in Adrienne Parker, his father's personal assistant. Adrienne had willingly procured anything and everything Logan required, without question. If she thought he was an extension of his father's will, all the better. As to why she didn't discuss any of his requests with the old man, well, that was a mystery, but it saved him presenting the carefully crafted reasoning to the old man if he'd asked—and eased the risk that he couldn't fool him.

"Logan?" His father's PA smiled at him from the doorway. He needed to talk to her about her future with the company because she was extremely valuable. But not when he was so worn out. Today had been all about transferring leadership after yesterday's takeover, the office dead quiet on a Sunday.

"Hey, Adrienne."

"Long day."

"It has been. Thanks for coming in. Did you get my father's office packed up?" His dad wasn't allowed back in the building—ever.

"Done, and my pleasure. I arranged to have it couriered to him." She advanced into the room and set her hand on the back of a chair. The position artfully displayed her curvaceous body, something he absently noted before powering down his laptop.

"Would you like to get dinner?" She ran a hand through her long, blonde hair.

"Hmm? Oh, sorry, Adrienne. I was just wondering how I'd get home, let alone go someplace to eat. I'm pretty much worn out."

"I'd be happy to pick something up for you and bring it by. Drive you home, if you like."

Danger, Will Robinson. He blamed missing the signals on his fatigue, as well as his single-minded focus on saving the business and everyone affected by it, rather than seeing it all collapse. Never mind that there wasn't anyone else for him but Victoria. In any event, he hadn't picked up on Adrienne's interest.

Miss Parker had been so helpful because she'd read the writing on the wall—clever girl—and bet on the younger horse. Now she was coming to assert her claim and ride the winner.

Logan wasn't particularly vain. His mother had seen to that. But women had always come easy and he'd seen no need to turn them down, cutting a wide swathe. Before Victoria.

"No. But thanks." He waited and watched, wondering if she was as astute as he believed.

It took but a few seconds before she nodded, only a slight tightening around her eyes betraying her state of mind. Not like Victoria who wore her feelings openly.

"Did you call off your wedding because of your plan to take over from your father?"

He supposed he owed her some sort of explanation. "Something like that."

"But you're not… I mean, are you reconsidering that action?"

"My next project."

"I see." She arranged her face in a professional smile. "Can we set up a time to meet about my future here?"

Adrienne either knew when to cut her losses or had only been interested in a brief fling. He didn't care, either way, but he'd know not to turn his back on her. "I'd already decided on finding a time tomorrow. Your aid didn't go unnoticed."

"I'll see you then." She moved gracefully toward the door, still poised and working her tight skirt for all it was worth. Letting him know what he was missing out on. Except his real loss had taken place three weeks, six days and some hours ago, and only one woman could assuage it.

He'd found out where Victoria had gone. Social media was a wonderful tool when it wasn't a curse. He'd be in Boston on Wednesday and nothing was going to get in his way, though he wondered if dealing with his father would turn out to be easy by comparison.

Chapter Five

"I wish you could stay longer." Victoria heard herself, whining like a toddler.

"I've been here the two days, Tori. Well, two days if you don't consider the time you spent on the phone with the office and the emergency trips to address 'issues' there." Her mom folded another item for her suitcase.

"I know. But if I screw this up Jon will replace me. In a heartbeat."

"And I appreciate that. I didn't expect you to dedicate all your time to me. I came to visit because I needed to know you were okay."

Something in her mother's tone indicated her hopes hadn't been realized. "I'm fine, Mom."

"You're a shadow of your former self. You've always been driven, but seriously, Tori. If I didn't know better, I'd think you were pregnant with the way you avoid food."

Her head spun and she stared blankly at her mother. "I'm not pregnant." *Logan's baby, someone to lavish all my unrequited love on.* She snapped out of it. Not a way to burden a child.

"I know you're not."

"How do you know?" It was stupid to continue in this vein, but she was curious.

"I know when you have your periods. I lived with you. So unless you've been with someone else since … well, you're not pregnant."

"Oh. Right." She pretended the conversation wasn't bothering her. She and Logan planned to have children, but it was a blessing that she wasn't carrying his child. He'd be forced into her life because of parenthood. And she'd be a shitty mother anyhow.

"I think you should come home."

"What? No. I'm fine."

"You need your family to take care of you."

"Mom, I'm twenty-eight. I've been taking care of myself for a long time."

"And doing a terrible job of it recently. You're going to fall prey to some bizarre virus and won't have the reserves to fight it."

There was no dealing with her mother when that woman got such things in her head. "I'll start. Today."

"How?"

"I'll have lunch with you before your plane leaves. And I'll buy more food for here."

"You'll eat?" Margaret's voice was infused with doubt.

"I will. I can't afford any more clothes so I'll have to eat my way back into the ones I own."

It was doubtful her mom put a lot of faith in her promise, but Victoria vowed she would try. If she became ill, everything she'd worked for would crumble. Mother's wisdom made sense.

The drive to the airport was quiet. She really didn't want her mother to leave, and she knew her parent was thinking dark thoughts, primarily because she was worried.

"Logan has taken over his father's business and from what Robert said, the elder Mr. Doherty is out of a job." Her mom didn't think much of Logan's dad, and only her good manners had kept things civil around him.

Why was her mom bringing this up now? "I know."

Her mother twisted to face her, and Victoria shot her a glance before returning her attention to the road.

She rarely drove the company car, stored in the underground parking lot, and it had far more power than her own.

"Have you been in contact? Did you talk to him?"

"No. I inadvertently saw it on the news."

"I see." Her mother's disappointment was clear.

"He has someone." Saying it out loud made her breathless, a kind of floating sensation that didn't marry well with driving.

"You saw *that* on the news?"

Caught. *Damn.* "I searched for the article, and there she was, all cozied up tight with him. She's the kind of woman he was always featured with."

"You know better than to believe everything the media says."

That was true. But it didn't matter anyhow, despite the fact her mom was still entertaining some kind of strange hope she and Logan would talk. "We'll stop at Dino's. I hear it has good food and it's close to the airport."

"That sounds nice."

Victoria ate her salad, spearing the shrimp with grim intent and choking them down. The greens were fresh and succulent and doused with a dressing she used to favor, but it took additional effort to swallow them. Her mother worked her way through a grilled chicken breast and a massive side order of fries—her guilty pleasure, and one Victoria knew she didn't indulge in very often.

"Are you okay?" Margaret gestured at her plate.

"I'm not very hungry," she admitted. "But I'll eat three squares, Mom. I promise. I don't want to get sick and I don't want you worrying."

"I always worry, even when there's nothing to worry about." Her mother contemplated the dessert menu and Victoria groaned inwardly. Her meal, far larger than anything she'd consumed in … close to four weeks or so sat uncomfortably in her belly.

"I'll have coffee," she said.

"There's some sherbet, nice and light. We'll both have a bowl."

It was like she was a little kid again with Mommy deciding for her. She bit her lip. Her mom was leaving and she'd miss everything about her in no time. "Sure."

Over a spoonful of the cool, light confection, Margaret said, "I found your ring."

"What?" Bombarded by the recollection of her engagement ring bouncing away from the trash can momentarily transfixed her, and the sherbet slipped off the spoon into the bowl. She stared after it and drifted again. Somehow that tenuous connection between the dessert and the curved utensil became vastly important, and she set the spoon down with a shaking hand. It clattered against the china.

"Tori? Honey, I'm sorry. I said I wouldn't talk about him."

With an effort, she looked up and tried a smile that didn't cling any better than the sherbet. "It's okay. Just tell me that it'll get better."

"You haven't been able to put it away after all. I think that's for the best."

"And feeling like someone just jumped on my chest is a good thing?" Her lunch roiled ominously and she swallowed against a rush of saliva. Weren't mothers supposed to soothe their children?

"Tori. Of course, it's not a good thing, but it only gets better when you separate out how you're feeling. Your father humiliated me. He took a shot at the core of who I was as a woman. No longer fertile. Unable to produce a son." Her mom's full lips, so like her own, set in a thin, hard line before relaxing into a laugh. "At first, even knowing it was his fault—if blame was to be assigned—didn't help. I was too ashamed.

"Once a little time had passed and people supported me, not to mention having three children to raise without their father, I came to accept the truth. It wasn't about me. My pride was bruised, for certain, and I missed him. We'd been married for over fifteen years. But the horrible things he said, the way he treated you especially... I discovered I didn't love him, or at least not the person he had become. People change, but your father took that to the extreme."

It wasn't the same, at least it didn't feel the same, but perhaps it was too soon. Victoria said, "So I'll get over this in time. Logan humiliated me and hurt my pride so once I recover from that—"

It was as ludicrous as it sounded, spoken at a table for two in a nice restaurant. She loved Logan, no matter how much he'd changed, no matter what he'd done, and a yawning, black cavern opened up inside to fill with despair. She'd never get over him, so begging people to reassure her was a useless endeavor. A person couldn't wallow and hide, however, without starving to death. She had financial obligations, so she'd be grateful she had her career. She glanced at her watch. "We need to get going."

"Honey—"

"Not helping, Mom."

"He hasn't given up."

She wasn't interested in how her mother knew that. She. Was. Not. Fumbling for her wallet, she tugged out a credit card and looked around for the waiter.

"I was trying to explain that this wasn't about you. Delores—"

Cutting her mom off, she said, "It's been a

month. I had the bandage in place. Don't you understand? It doesn't matter what Delores says or what explanation Logan comes up with—even if I should happen to hear it. Nothing is going to take away what he did, what it did to me. You'll have to be disappointed, Mom. In me. Because I'm simply not capable of trusting that man again, regardless of how he envisions connecting with me. It was all or nothing."

Her mother's face drained of color, and her eyes filled with tears before she looked away. She might have said something else, but the server arrived and both of them recovered in the time it took to sort out the bill.

Small talk filled the awkward silence right up to the flight being called, and Victoria forced herself to set her negative emotions aside. They weren't really directed at her mother, despite the woman's probing of the mortal wound.

"Thanks for coming. I've missed you. Come again when you can."

"I will."

Victoria doubted it.

"I love you, Tori."

With a final hug, her mom's small form passed through security, and Victoria wanted to run after her. She wasn't sure if it was because she needed her mom to stay or if she needed to follow.

Emotionally drained, she trudged out to her vehicle, parked in the short-term lot. She sat for a while, her head tilted against the side window. At least she'd had nearly two days with her mom, despite the interruptions of the office, without a mention of the one person who had spoiled the past couple of hours—in absentia. It would suck if she became this despondent each and every time she saw her family, being reminded of him. Even by them.

Slapping the steering wheel, she set her teeth. Hadn't she promised herself she wasn't going to allow him to impact her precious family? He wasn't going to leave her with nothing.

She drove back to work, struggled through finding someplace to park, and was in her usual focused frame of mind when she arrived.

"Victoria! Did your mom get away all right?" Dawna beamed at her and passed over a file.

"She did. It was great to have her here."

"Too short a visit with one's mom. I know how much I miss mine."

Guilt lashed with Dawna's innocent comment, and all she could do was nod. "What's this?"

"The Tattered Bride spread. Some report from marketing."

Crap. "Okay. Thanks. Anything else?"

"Nope. It's all under control. You've whipped this place into shape. Mr. Crisp spun his wheels." Dawna winked bawdily, her entire face screwing up. "He was all talk, no action."

"Thanks for the vote of confidence. I know I've pushed people."

"You have, and they needed it. They all speculated, you know. About you coming here right off … right from the not getting married thing. Whether you'd be able to handle the job or fall apart."

Victoria had heard some of the speculative thinking, shut down when she approached. At least only Jason had thought to take advantage of the jilted woman. As for falling apart, she'd heard them talk about her overcompensating. She smiled, the conversation with her mother having numbed her to any impact of the personal comment. "I'm sure they did. But we're headed for the black and I plan to keep us going in that direction."

"So you're staying on?" Curiosity and happiness vied on Dawna's pleasant features.

Was she? She'd stay wherever Logan—and his blondes—weren't. "Could be."

Settling behind her desk, she opened the file, her brow furrowing. The book-cover option had been picked up—for a comic book? She dropped the papers and shoved them away. What in hell? Laughter bubbled in her throat, making her ears pop and then escaped, a bitter caw filling the room. She could see it now, some graphic artist making a parody of her baby. Big boobs spilling over the torn bodice, puffy lips and heavily-lined eyes staring from the pages. Probably blood and gore too.

She reached for the phone. "Marketing. Jill speaking."

"It's Victoria Sparrow. I'm looking at the book option offer for The Tattered Bride."

"Isn't it incredible? It was a difficult sell for a romance though we tried."

Victoria pressed a fist against her sternum. "True, but—"

"We had a few pubs inquire, the ones who publish horror, dystopian. You know. But this offer blew us away. We closed a few hours ago."

It was within marketing's rights to close the deal. Victoria had granted them license to do so after the other options had gone so well. But... "I don't know as I'm comfortable with the sale."

"Uh, want to talk to Barry?" Barry Walker, the head of the department.

What would she say? Staring at the rendering, she decided. "No. I'll have to learn to let go." Truer words...

"Oh, right. I know. We get attached to our creations. A couple of weeks and she'll be out there,

Victoria."

Mustering an enthusiasm she didn't feel, she replied. "For sure. And thanks."

She applied herself during the rest of the day, her gaze straying to the file sitting squarely on the top left-hand corner of her desk until she stuffed it into a drawer. This time she wouldn't give in to following up on it via a search, instead, would watch for the perfume advert and some of the others. It'd be fine.

Dawna poked her head in. "It's nearly six and I'm heading out. You?"

"Shortly." Her promise to her mother flickered in her head. She had to pick up some food items. "See you tomorrow."

The older woman's face creased with concern. "I hoped a couple of days with your mom would have eased some of that strain, Victoria. But you look even more stressed."

She touched her cheek and forced a smile. "Do I look that bad?"

"Not bad. You're beautiful. But you're carrying a big load. Best you cut back on your hours—and eat better."

At least the woman didn't tell her she needed to get more sleep. "I'll take that into consideration."

Staring at her computer screen didn't inspire her, so about ten minutes later, she packed up and headed for the same grocery store. Sacks in hand, she drove home, curiously reluctant to do so. Maybe she should … what? Go for a drink someplace with friends? She didn't have any here, having had no time to make any, and had been reluctant to schmooze with staff in the early days.

She thought longingly of her friends back home. Most were Logan's and therefore out of bounds, but Theresa and Kaitlyn were still connected. They had respected her request for space right after that awful day because she'd taken refuge with her family—and in her work.

Both had been hurt and confused when she'd left town without sharing but had forgiven her, as good friends do, apparently. She wasn't sure she deserved it, especially as she'd left them with horribly expensive bridesmaid gowns. At least they were suitable to wear out as cocktail dresses. She made up her mind to call them both tonight, maybe even a conference call, or Facetime. Brief emails and shorter texts hadn't done more than ensure a slender thread of connection.

She could reassure them that she was doing fine and staying in Boston so they could consider coming to see her. The idea of living here and planning for loved ones to visit surely was a signal she was building a new life for herself. Contrary to the body blows she'd received today. Right?

Emilio had been replaced by Gordon, a fellow she didn't know and didn't care to make the effort to. A hulk of a man, he frowned at everyone, and other than that, didn't acknowledge them. Emerging from the parking garage entrance, she strode past him, and was surprised when he called out her name.

"Yes?"

"There's someone waiting for you." He gestured toward the lobby.

"Oh. Okay. Thanks." She reversed direction and headed there, hefting her shopping. Gordon wouldn't have let just anyone in, even to wait.

She wasn't prepared when Logan's tall frame unfolded upward from one of the chairs. Numb, her fingers uncurled and the handle of the sacks slipped through them to hit the tiles with a dull thump. Her case and purse followed, and she couldn't summon the wherewithal to even make a futile grab for them.

Three orange orbs rolled across her peripheral vision and she watched the fruit cluster at Logan's feet. He wore his usual casual apparel, well-worn jeans that cost more than an average person's monthly rent and a button-down shirt beneath a soft leather jacket he must have donned in deference to Boston's weather.

Neither seemed to be capable of speech, and she struggled to be the first. To shut him down. "This isn't happening."

She squatted to pick up her laptop and purse, abandoning the groceries. The thought of gathering them up and letting him see her trembling hands would add insult to injury. Upright and turning on her heel in the next second, she hustled toward Gordon.

The guard was standing at attention, watching intently, and she suddenly valued his lack of interaction as much as she intuited his now apparent resolve to protect the building's tenants. She moved past him, picking up his barely audible, "Sorry, Miss,", before he put himself between her and Logan who was hard on her heels.

"Victoria! Please, baby. Give me a minute. Please."

No minutes. Not a second. She'd given him everything and there was nothing left. Refusing to reply, she gained the elevator and pressed so hard on the button she snapped her fingernail off. The car arrived instantly, something in her favor for a change, and she stepped inside.

Without a glance at the tussle taking place in the lobby, she punched her floor number—and the one above. The doors inched closed and she leaned against the wall, her knees like water.

Too fucking much. His appearance was etched on

the back of her eyelids, so she popped them open, only to see his face in her mind's eye. He'd been alone, or at least she hadn't seen anyone else, though likely a herd of dancing elephants could have been present and she wouldn't have noticed.

Hurrying down the hall to her door, she somehow found the keys and let herself in. Throwing deadbolt offered her a measure of relief, though she wasn't afraid of Logan. Terrified of herself, yes. Her immediate reaction had been to throw herself into his arms, the ones he'd opened to her. Finding the ability to protect herself came from a place she hadn't known existed.

Feeling lightheaded and panting as though she'd run miles, she set her stuff down and stumbled to the kitchen. The wine she and her mom hadn't finished was still on the counter, a robust red, with maybe a third left in the bottle.

Grabbing a water glass, she filled it and took a great gulp of the beverage. Another followed, and by the third, she thought maybe she wouldn't fall on her face. Her nerves steadied and she could breathe again. She filled the glass with the rest of the wine.

She went to sit on the couch, drawing her legs beneath her, and considered that she hadn't handled the meeting very well. Meeting? Well, it hadn't been a confrontation. Logan hadn't given off any hostile vibes and she strove not to interpret the look on his face and in his eyes...

What did he want, that he'd come to Boston? *You. He wants you.* She stomped her hopeful heart into submission and summoned up her nasty voice. Logan had her and threw her away. There was no freaking way he'd get the chance again. She didn't care what he wanted.

Throwing back half of her drink, she nearly

choked and then sipped at the rest. A firm knock at the door made her jump, and she watched the panels in wary fascination. Did the handle turn? Another knock, this one louder. She shoved to her feet, wavering.

"Who is it?"

"Gordon Perrault. From downstairs."

She ventured closer, lightheaded from too much alcohol, too quickly, on her empty stomach. Because that's all it was. "What do you want?"

"To apologize again. He said he was your fiancée and had forgotten his key." The words were a little muffled, but she heard them.

She cautiously threw the locks and opened the door. Gordon looked sheepish and very apologetic. She figured he was afraid of losing his job. Holding onto the door for support, she said, "Don't let him in again. Or anyone I don't put on the list."

"I won't. But he showed me pictures of you. Both of you. Together. You looked like a couple." He sat bags of groceries inside.

Ignoring the storm of emotion his words set off in her, she asked, "He's gone?"

"Yes. Not willingly. I had to, uh, well, he's a scrapper."

Logan? She knew he was in good shape, worked out and took care of his body, but she didn't think he knew how to fight. "He fought?"

Gordon shrugged. "He didn't want to leave until he spoke with you. I figured you didn't want that to happen. Do you have a restraining order?"

"No. What did you do to him?" Yep, she was the crazy one. Worried about the man who'd wrecked her.

"A shot to the ribs and one to the kidney settled him down. I put him in a cab. He can go to Emerg if he thinks he needs to. And you should think about that restraining order if you don't want him to come after you again. He's obsessed. I know that look."

Shock had her nodding and backing away, closing the door on yet another apology. She relocked it on autopilot and wandered to her bedroom. Confused and worried, she stripped off her suit and underwear and left them in a crumpled heap on the floor. Ignoring her nighttime routine, she clambered into bed, naked, in full makeup and without brushing her teeth.

Her stomach growled once before the wine eased her under.

****

"You can wrap one of those elastic bandages around your ribs for comfort if you like, Mr. Doherty. We don't treat bruised ribs like we used to, but sometimes the support helps." The ER doctor made a note on the chart. "I expect you might see some evidence of blood in your urine for the next couple of days, but unless it intensifies don't worry. The scan didn't flag any actual injury, merely localized bruising. But come back immediately if you're concerned."

"Thanks." *Merely.* Logan wouldn't have bothered seeing a doctor, except he needed to be sure he was well before his next contact with Victoria.

"You might want to steer clear of bar fights." There wasn't a hint of censure in the man's voice, nor any humor. Logan supposed they saw far worse here.

"I will." He hadn't exactly told them the truth. Being beaten up had been humbling enough, but telling them he'd been trying to get past a security guard to his fiancée might have resulted in them calling the authorities. A bar fight sounded manly. He wanted to laugh at himself, but he kept seeing Victoria's expression.

Her pallor frightened him, and the hurt in her

eyes… The sight of his woman had stolen his speech. Her beautiful hair shorn, her face and body so thin… But it was the look on her face, part shock, part horror and … pain.

The doctor's voice interrupted his reverie. He supposed he should be thankful, although he deserved to hurt at the memory, too.

"Excuse me?"

"An over-the-counter painkiller is indicated. See your regular doctor in a week."

"Thanks." He threw the hospital gown on the bed, wincing with the movement and decided to invest in several of those elastic bandages. His right side above his ass sported a rapidly darkening red bruise. At least his face had escaped the damage, because that he couldn't hide when he publicly stalked Victoria.

The guard had called him obsessed and that hit the nail on the head. He'd caused Victoria's pain and somehow he was going to erase it.

Part of his plan was unfolding and her having a welter-weight champion at her apartment building door was an oversight, or he'd have made greater strides tonight. Selecting a credit card, he made his way toward the cashier. He'd only begun to pay, and while his finances might be finite, the currency in his heart was not.

Chapter Six

She squinted at the clock. The hour should have struck panic into her heart but instead, there was only a muted lurch. Dawna would be in the office by now, and wondering where Victoria was. First in, last out—that had been her routine for the past month. Even the cleaning staff knew her by name.

She wasn't thinking about those few minutes in the lobby last night. Instead, she focused on the danger of becoming dependent on alcohol. The tumblers of wine, consumed in such a short period of time without any food to soak it up had given her a long, restful sleep. That alone numbed her to the warning of drinking too much.

Her cell rang, out in the living room, and she contemplated the distance to where it reposed in her purse. It wasn't worth it, and she closed her eyes. It rang again, and she grudgingly felt her way to the edge of the mattress. Swiveling her feet to the floor, she heaved her torso upright and nearly fell on her face.

"Geez." Her lips felt chapped and she had a slight headache. Had to have been the wine and not the bizarre scenario in the lobby—nope, she wasn't thinking about that.

Nude, she shivered her way to locate her cell, dragging it from the depths of her bag. Two missed calls from Dawna. Reluctantly, she called the woman back, deciding to take a sick day. There was another bottle of wine, unopened, and she needed her rest.

"Victoria? Are you okay?"

Wincing at the shrill voice, she held the phone away. "I'm not feeling very well. I slept through the alarm." She didn't even know how to set the alarm on her phone but it sounded good.

"Oh, dear. Something you ate? The flu? You don't sound stuffed up. What can I do?"

Something she knew. Someone. Victoria pinched her thigh. "Probably flu. I don't think I'll be in today."

"You mustn't be feeling well. But best you stay home if you're contagious. I can bring you soup?"

She nearly laughed. Contagious. "I have what I need here, thanks." Although the thought of red wine for breakfast…

"Would you like me to send some of these flowers over? To cheer you up?"

"Flowers?" It wasn't unheard of for clients to send a bouquet as a thank you. "From who?"

"I haven't a clue. There's no note. Not with any of them. But there have to be a dozen bouquets. Red roses with baby's breath. Stunning."

She gripped the phone in a suddenly sweaty palm. Her voice wouldn't work.

"Victoria? Are you there?"

"Uh huh. I'm here. And no, don't send the flowers. The scent will be too much for me. In fact, get rid of them."

"All those beautiful blooms?"

"All of them. Give them away, throw them up. Out. Whatever."

"I'll deal with it. You take care and I'll check with you later."

"I'll call *you*. In case I'm asleep."

Setting the cell on the coffee table, she became aware of how chilled she was and rushed to grab a robe. Detouring into the bathroom, she surveyed the damage in the mirror as she used the facilities and shrugged. The scarecrow look suited her mood.

Ignoring the beckoning bottle of wine, she put a pot of coffee on and rummaged in the fridge for the alcoholic creamer. Compromise was a good thing. While the coffee dripped, she dragged out her laptop and searched restraining orders. Oh, she knew she'd never apply for one, because Logan was no risk to her, not physically, but she wondered about the language involved. Because she knew she'd better have the verbiage when she next saw him. That man never gave up on anything in his life.

Well, he'd given up on their marriage, but besides that. Not when it came to him getting his own way. How was it that she'd never found that quality distasteful before? She shut her inner voice down before it came up with a positive—and unpalatable answer. *Because he was never wrong that you noticed—fair, and kind and loving—and it was always in your best interest.* Tapping through a menu, she frowned. She had no control, not even over her own damn inner voice.

Was he hurting today? Did he seek medical care? She was too tired to be angry with him and her worry leaked through. Though she'd beat him with one of those bouquets if she saw him again. Which wasn't going to happen. *Restraining Orders. Where to apply. Information required.*

With a shuddering sigh, she clicked out of the screen and then went and poured a coffee, doctoring it with the creamy booze. She took a swallow. Nectar of the gods. It didn't influence her predicament, however, and she couldn't sit on it very long. Meaning, she couldn't hide in this apartment for however long it took Logan to give up.

Pinching the bridge of her nose between thumb and forefinger, she considered her options and snatched up her cell.

"Robert Vermette." Her brother-in-law's voice was clogged with sleep and she did the math. He and Paige would still be enjoying the last hour of slumber before the morning rush of getting the kids ready and off to daycare yanked them into wakefulness. Victoria decided she didn't much care if she'd robbed him.

"It's Victoria. Logan's here."

Two beats of quiet, then, "I see."

"What's your advice?"

"Legal or otherwise?"

"I'll listen to both." The booze must be making her magnanimous.

"You can obtain a restraining or—"

"I know. I know. And embarrass myself, waste a whole lot of time, and end up with bad publicity. Logan would never harm me. But he needs to stay away."

"I don't think that's going to happen."

"You know more than you're saying."

"Privileged."

Holy shit. Robert blew it, and deliberately because he'd never risk it with anyone he didn't trust. He could get thrown in front of the bar association. He was bound to avoid even announcing an affiliation with Logan. "I see."

She desperately wanted to know the capacity in which Logan had employed him when it hit her between the eyes. Robert would never take her ex on as a client unless the reasoning was such that he couldn't refuse. Thoughts and impressions teemed through her brain in never-ending streams, and she wished she hadn't emptied half the damn bottle into her cup. Nothing fell into line to explain anything, but all the conclusions she'd drawn from the pictures and news articles crumbled beneath the onslaught.

"Victoria?"

"I'm trying to think."

"Give him ten minutes to explain. That's my advice. Even five."

The entire unwieldy structure she'd built over the past month creaked alarmingly and shifted. She put up a mental hand to shore it up and gritted her teeth. "I can't."

"Why?"

"I can't let myself hear it."

"Oh, Victoria. No. Logan had his back against the wall. Nothing like that will ever happen again. He'll never hurt you like that."

"I can't. I can't do it." And she couldn't. "Thanks, Robert, and sorry I woke you."

"Victoria."

She was going to change her name to something like … Mud. "Give my love to Paige and the kids."

So she was a coward, no surprise. When the going got tough—personally … emotionally—Victoria Sparrow took off running or hid behind a cleverly constructed edifice only she was allowed to live inside. And understand, apparently.

As if by magic—or by interfering brother-in-law—her cell rang. "Hey, Mom. Up early?"

"Robert called."

"Right."

"Grow a pair and see him, Tori. Talk to Logan."

Grow a pair? Was her mother on social media again? Watching sitcoms? "I can't."

"I know it's scary. It challenges how you've operated most of your life, and damned if I could make you do it any differently then."

Damn Mother's wisdom. "I have to go, Mom. I'm late for work."

Her mother was silent, only the faint noises of apartment sounds permeated Victoria's hearing, those and the pounding of her heart. "Think about it, honey."

"Okay." Her mother always knew when she was lying so it was all right to say it.

None the wiser as to how she was going to deal with him, she went to take a long, hot bath. Lying in the tub, bubbles popping softly around her and the soothing scent of lavender wafting through the steamy air, she drifted until the water cooled, thinking about precisely nothing.

Clean and refreshed, she toweled off and wandered back to bed. Curling up beneath the linens, she cautiously switched her brain back on. The good night's sleep hadn't done a thing to give her any new ideas, but she could at least take today.

The intercom buzzed, and she set a pillow over her head. With her luck, Dawna would have disregarded her request and be at the door with soup. It buzzed again, and she tossed the cushion aside, glaring. Fumbling back into her robe, she stalked over and pressed the button. "Yes?"

"Delivery for you, Mizz Sparrow." Emilio's cheerful voice didn't make her smile. What was he doing working on a Thursday?

"Why are you on the door?"

"Brett called in sick and we're down to four days a week at the plant."

It was ludicrous to have a conversation with that nice man who was finding it difficult to make ends meet. "Just a delivery?"

"Yes, ma'am."

"I'll get it tomorrow."

"Probably best if I brought it up today."

Was it something alive? Like more freaking flowers? A puppy? She'd always wanted a dog, and Logan had promised—argh! She was going insane.

"What is it?"

"Brunch."

Brunch. "Who sent it?" Like she didn't know.

"It doesn't say."

The press and release thing on the intercom was making her tired. She pushed the button one last time—she hoped. "I'll come get it."

Fitting her breasts into a bra, she pulled a t-shirt over her head before stepping into fresh underwear and a pair of yoga pants. Finding her keys and a five-dollar bill, she caught the elevator to the lobby, where Emilio waited with an enormous box and an equally big smile on his face.

"Taking a day off?"

"No. I'm not feeling well."

"Then you should have let me bring this to you!"

"It's fine. Seriously." She slipped the five into his hand—he always protested at anything larger—and hefted the box. Something cushioned reposed inside and she indeed could smell food.

"It's from one of the best restaurants in Boston," he confided. "I've never been, but I've heard about it."

She knew Logan was the sender, but there wasn't a garbage can big enough in the area to stuff the damn thing into it. How did he know she wasn't at work? "Share it with me then."

"Oh, I can't do that."

"You can." She looked around and marched the box over to his desk.

He stood awkwardly for a moment and then hurried to pull his chair out for her. She sat and commenced the opening of brunch while he dragged a stool over.

"Don't look so anxious, Emilio. If someone comes, deal with them. I thought you said it was quiet most mornings once people have gone to work."

"It is. But this isn't … I mean you're my boss. Well, not exactly, but…"

"Eat." She'd dug the covered dishes out of the heated knapsack and peeled the tops off. Eggs benedict, hash browns, toast, a side order of crisp bacon and a sealed thermos of lattes. Real cutlery was wrapped in fabric napkins and the plates and cups were actual china. No wonder the thing weighed a ton.

"Do you eat like this all the time?" Emilio gingerly took a serving and tasted the eggs.

"No. This is my version of comfort food." *Damn you, Logan.* She wasn't going to let the memories get to her.

"You need comfort?"

"Apparently so."

Her appetite surprisingly came back, enough to eat one egg on a half slice of toast, a spoonful of potatoes, and two strips of the bacon. The latte was perfect and she sipped with her eyes closed.

"It's working. The comfort thing." Emilio beamed at her. "You look comforted."

If only it was as easy as that. Food, Mother Nature's anti-depressant. Too close to Mother's wisdom. "I'm feeling better," she allowed.

"Did he hurt you?" Wide face flushing, the man looked away. "Gordon told me you had a stalker. I've been watching for him."

Great. Logan could get creamed by her favorite guard, too. "He left me at the altar."

Crazy, but telling Emilio her awful secret didn't elicit an iota of shame. Maybe he already knew.

"Stupido."

"Or smart."

He furrowed his brow. "Smart?"

She shrugged and began to stack the empty containers and plates. "He's a wealthy, important man and I'm … pretty ordinary."

"Wealth and power don't mean a good person. And I do not think you are ordinary, not one bit."

She gave him a smile. "Oh, he's a good person. Pretty wonderful, actually."

"Not if he left you at the altar." His eyes flashed and he fisted his hands.

Touched by his fierce defense, she said, "He left me for a reason, Emilio."

"What was that reason?"

"I don't know, actually, he wouldn't tell me. But it would have been a good one." And now she was feeling that sad mix of emotions. Worthless, unimportant, lacking…

Emilio distracted her. "If you chose him and you say he is all those good things, then the reason was something he couldn't tell you."

"We told one another everything." A shard of pain caught in the back of her throat.

"That might be so, but there are times when a man cannot share. At least not right away. Maybe never."

She stared at the security guard. "How can that be? If not with the woman you … you love, then…"

He shook his head. "Forgive me. I shouldn't be so pushy. My wife says I am bossy."

"You have a right to your opinion. I asked."

"I'll clear this away, Mizz Sparrow." He stood and tucked in the edges of the box. Then, looking everywhere but at her, he said, "Sometimes it is in the best interest of others to keep certain things to oneself. I might have withheld from my wife on occasion, as well."

She couldn't process the conversation and blamed it on too much cholesterol. Gesturing at the box, she asked, "What will you do with all of this?"

"I'll send it back to the restaurant. The arrangements were made."

"Oh, okay. Thanks."

"Thank you for sharing your food. My Gianna has never prepared the eggs benedict."

Full but hardly contented, she went back upstairs, thinking hard about Emilio's sage words. Logan had indeed withheld, but she'd attributed it to his reluctance to make it worse. So his reluctance to share was somehow related to… She didn't have a clue what it related to.

Okay, take the wedding out of the picture. Would he have told her in private? If he could? Maybe so. Her emotions had run rampant—she didn't blame herself for that—and she had lashed out, pushed him away, because of the circumstances. He'd appeared honestly remorseful and his mother had cried. His father had smiled. Did *they* know beforehand?

She paced to the window and stared down at the street and then up at the sky. Logan hadn't been prepared. He was *always* prepared. If he'd come to the conclusion that they weren't meant to be as a couple, it would not have been at the actual wedding ceremony. Cold feet for Logan meant days before. She thought. But maybe she was wrong. Maybe she didn't know him the way she thought. They shared everything important with one another. She thought.

Her head ached. What could be so awful that he couldn't tell her and made him call off the wedding? *You.* Her nasty voice spoke up.

Except it kept coming back to the timing. She dared, for the first time, to consider that he hadn't ditched her because she wasn't enough for him. So was it good timing for him to tell her now? What was so special about now?

He had only taken over the company a couple of days earlier after what had to have been a pitched battle with his father. He wasn't fighting one when they were together. He hadn't been in contact with her all of that time after the non-wedding, at least not directly, though that would have been different had she gone home to sleep. He'd been in her house, probably at night. Oh, he'd left voice mails, sent texts, but she hadn't read them. He asked her mother tell her to wait. Robert had asked that she wait. She wished she'd read the damn note.

There were a lot of clues, yet she couldn't connect the dots. Where was her vaunted intelligence? Logan had obviously waited until after the takeover to come to her directly. She couldn't help but smirk a little at the thought of old man Doherty out in the cold. He'd been nasty to her—to most everyone—calling her a gold digger, insinuating she'd demand a part of the business. She'd appeased him, so as not to create a wider rift between him and Logan, by signing off, but he still didn't like her. If she was married to Logan maybe she wouldn't have seen anything of him.

Smiles. She touched her lips, tracing the curve. Sean had smirked when she'd stalked out of the church. Not as in pleasure, but maybe satisfaction, like he'd obtained his own way? Or wasn't that the same thing?

"I don't know!" she shouted, and was glad her neighbors weren't home.

"Okay. If I'm not deluding myself, Logan made a snap judgment in calling off the wedding. Like a fairly instantaneous one, because he'd have contacted me during the few hours we were apart before the ceremony." While she had her hair done and a manicure and a pedicure. She would have answered any call from him, right up to the minute she left her purse in the car and went into the church.

"It's something he learned right before, but from who?" No one answered, not even her inside voice.

That smirk on Sean's face kept flashing in the back of her mind, but she didn't focus on the obvious criminal, scanning her memory banks for anyone else who might have dropped a bombshell beforehand. David had flown in the night before and after renewing their acquaintance, they enjoyed one another's company. It was doubtful he'd have something to force Logan to jilt her.

Patrick and his wife, Josey, were the couple they spent the most time with, and there had never been any animosity where they were concerned. The minister? A close friend of her mother's, Father Cedric, wouldn't have any reason to interfere.

She wished she could ask—grabbing her phone, she dialed. Voicemail. "Robert? Please call when you get this."

Making the bed and straightening her room didn't make the time go quicker. Neither did cleaning the bathroom. She could call her mother, but she'd been with Victoria at the back of the church. Her sisters and her friends might have seen something, but they'd preceded her by only moments. When her phone signaled she was on it.

"Hello?"

"It's Robert."

"I have a question."

"I might not be able to answer."

"I think you can. Remember the church?"

"Not something I'm likely to forget."

She'd thought carefully about the parameters of what she wanted to ask. "Who was the last person from the congregation to speak to Logan?"

Without hesitation, he replied, "His father. Sean was nearly late and came up to shake Logan's hand. He spoke in his ear for a time."

"Thank you."

"Victoria?"

"It's on me now, Robert. And only if I can manage my inadequacies."

"Which are only in your mind, as powerful as that might make them, sister-in-law."

She snorted, an extremely unladylike sound. "I don't know what I did to deserve such a wonderful family, which includes you—and Michael."

"I ask myself that often when I consider how I've been included in yours."

She wanted to weep. "Stop the sweet talk. For now. I love you, Robert, as a brother-in-law."

"And I, you. Victoria. Know you can trust Logan. Rely on that."

"I'm not promising anything."

"I have faith in you. And I tire of this weight I'm carrying. Your sister is like a persistent drip of water against stone with her incessant prying."

"Sure, make this about you and your burden of confidentiality. Paige must suspect something."

"She saw Logan and me together."

"Uh oh."

"Indeed. But I'll withstand it. She trusts me."

"Ouch. I hear you. Thanks, Robert."

She knew his number but couldn't make herself dial it. Her reasoning wasn't faulty, she didn't think, but why hadn't he told her what his father said? She would have helped…

Hand at her mouth, the only conclusion she could come to took her breath. Sean had made Logan promise not to tell her or else… She had no idea what nefarious consequences that man had threatened, but it boiled down to him. If she was even on the right path.

Where would Logan be? She picked up her cell and began to enter his number and then canceled it. This wasn't something she could do over the phone, and she felt him close by.

Making her decision, she shrugged into a jacket and found a pair of shoes. Tucking her phone inside a pocket, she grabbed some cash and her keys. She wasn't going far, merely taking a huge leap of faith.

"You okay going out there by yourself? I'd better get you a cab." Emilio rushed over.

"It's fine. Really."

He studied her and then nodded. "Okay. If you're sure."

"I'm certain." They had forged an interesting friendship over brunch and she hoped he would see his way clear and not make things awkward down the road. Like put up a wall between them because he was a "mere" security guard. With great insight of the human dynamic.

Stepping out onto the sidewalk, she stood there, waiting. This wasn't exactly the paper-bag princess style, but she wasn't the tattered bride either. Her fingers flew to her hair. Clean, but awry. No makeup, and her clothes... With a chuckle, she let it go.

****

It was fucking cold in Boston. Logan zipped his leather jacket, wished he had gloves, and figured he should pace the area around the bench. He was reluctant to go too far from it, having usurped the handy seating from a determined old man with several bags that took up the whole space. But his aching ribs and throbbing kidney area demanded a change in posture, so he pushed to his feet and carefully took a few steps.

Watching the front door of Victoria's apartment building wasn't something he'd ever thought probable, but it was part of the plan. He'd just moved it several dozen blocks when she didn't go into work. The flower delivery had gone smoothly, and he'd been on location bright and early, but no sign of her.

Redirecting her favorite food had taken a quick call, and he'd fondly imagined her calling him and inviting him to share. Instead, another really big security guy had schlepped the box out to a cab after an interminable wait. God, he was freezing out here. Maybe renting a limo would have been a better idea, because his thin California blood wasn't up to fall weather in Boston.

He made a careful left turn in deference to his ribs and saw her. A tall, thin figure dressed entirely in black. She several hundred yards away, but he knew her. His entire body knew her, his heart picking up the pace and his cock hardening.

Victoria just stood there, motionless, up against the building to the side of the door. He could reach her in moments. And if the big guy came out to whale on him, maybe she'd take pity.

His gait impaired by the soreness of his injuries, he nevertheless made steady progress across the street. The narrow corridor slowed the speed of the traffic as he wove his way to her. She saw him midway across, and stiffened, and then smiled. He followed that beacon, forced to dodge a couple of pedestrians who snarled his way in Boston's infamous accent, and then he was there. Right in front of her. Staring into her beautiful, blue eyes. Worry and longing warred with a hint of fear and his heart fucking well broke.

Carefully, he set his hands on either side of her face, cradling her delicate skull. The short, silky strands of her hair brushed against his skin. "Baby. I'm so sorry.

Can we talk?"

"There's a coffee shop across the street." She turned her cheek into his palm.

He longed for privacy but understood her caution. If he failed her again, she could flee and pull up the drawbridge. "Sure. Whatever you want."

Chapter Seven

It was insane, that after over a month of excoriating pain, held at bay only when she was able to immerse herself in work—and sometimes not even then—that she was face to face with the man who'd caused it. His beloved features were the same, albeit with a few more lines and a haunted look about his eyes. His dark hair was still well cut and drew attention to the beautiful shape of his head.

He seemed thinner, though the jacket masked his torso. She feasted her eyes without pause, knowing that the pending conversation could go either way, and she wanted one last look—in case.

"Are you okay?" she asked. "Gordon—the security guard, said…"

"I'm fine." He devoured her with his stare. "You look beautiful, baby."

She didn't demur. He'd always found her so, regardless of whether she'd come in from the garden a sweaty mess with dirt smudging her face or dressed to the nines with an expert application of makeup. Apparently, the "waif without makeup look" and her lack of professional attire was equally appealing. If she could believe him. If everything that took place between them before, was true.

"I missed you," he said. "Victoria, I love you so much."

She wanted to reply, badly, but fear paralyzed her vocal chords. Venturing a trembling smile, she let him take her hand. Her scalp still tingled from his gentle, yet possessive touch.

"Will you let me explain?"

"I'll listen."

"That's all I can ask, baby. I know I shattered you. I didn't have time to think, not even to come up with an excuse. And I didn't want to make something up, to lie to you. So I told you we couldn't get married."

"I thought it was about me." She had to say it. It felt as though she'd just ripped a flak jacket off and painted a target right on her chest, over her heart, but she had to take the risk with Logan. Because he knew he'd already taken a vital shot, and if he administered the coup de grace then so be it. Something had to give.

Squeezing her hand, he leaned closer, fixing her with his stare. She was mesmerized, as always by the tawny shade, and breathed in his familiar scent. Bergamot with earthier notes immersed her.

"There's nothing about you I don't want, Victoria, and everything I do. Know that. What I've wanted since our first date. Hell, probably since I laid eyes on you, but for sure once I got to know you. But … it was about you, in part. That old bastard."

"What?" It stung and nearly negated the preceding heartfelt words.

Logan rushed ahead, feeling her recoil. "My father wanted to choose my wife, to control me as he controls most everything else in his life. With the exception of my mother. And of late, my siblings."

"And he didn't see me as suitable."

"Of course not. You're too good for the likes of him. You have class, you're kind, you tell the truth, your family members care about one another, support each other, and you don't care about massive amounts of money."

Reeling, she blinked at him. "Wow."

"Exactly. He wanted someone like him, someone with no principles, no scruples, someone he could manipulate with money and power, seeing as he discovered I'm not amenable. My brother wants nothing to do with him—or the business—and my sisters had been letting me vote their stock now they've found the men of their dreams."

"But I signed off…"

"Not enough. Your loyalty was to me. The old man had someone lined up who would look to him."

"I saw her."

"You did? I didn't think you knew Lexie."

Who was Lexie? Probably another blonde with big boobs. "I meant Adrienne."

A hint of guilt flashed through his eyes and she tried to pull away. He spoke quickly. "If my father handpicked Adrienne, he badly misjudged. She chose sides early. I'll admit I found her assistance invaluable, and she'll be part of the company, but I'm not at all interested in her. If that's what you're thinking. She thought differently, but I corrected her assumption. There's only one woman in my life, if she'll have me."

She wanted him. Thinking that she'd lost him… "What did your father do, Logan?"

His eyes narrowed in anger and she felt the rage simmering in his tense form. "He made deals. With everyone cut from the same cloth as him. The couple of board members who saw a payout to their benefit. Other companies who'd like to absorb our subsidiaries, primarily overseas. Certain politicians. If I hadn't stopped the wedding, he'd have put his plan in motion right then and there, and Doherty Holdings would have collapsed. I wouldn't have been able to stop it. My father would be rolling in the proceeds as well as those board members. The stockholders would have been shafted, pennies on the dollar, and our staff, the workers, unemployed. No warning, no way to prepare."

"That's pure evil," she breathed, once it all sank in. "All because he didn't want you to marry me?"

"He's insane—or something close to it. Your brother-in-law suspects some form of mental illness, but I think it's just him. The way he is. As his youngest and the only one involved in the company, he was going to rule me by any means possible."

"And you couldn't share that with me?" She couldn't help but remember that devastating confrontation in the small room in the church.

"He'd have been able to tell, Victoria. He'd have put things into motion, knowing we'd simply postpone the wedding until I found a way around him. There's no way you could have hidden it from him, not with the way you wear your emotions on your face. That's why he wanted it called off there. I hated what I did, and if it was just about me, I wouldn't have hurt you like that. There wasn't an alternative. He was convinced—how could he not be after what I did—and it gave me the opportunity to dismantle his arrangements. It took time—"

He pleaded with his eyes for her to understand, but then surely he'd known she would. Logan knew her and she'd have called off the wedding herself if she'd known what old man Doherty had planned for all those people. She thought hateful things about the man and blessed the fact Delores was Logan's mother.

"It's like one of those medieval stories with the evil king and the hapless prince."

Logan laughed, easing some of the strain on his face, and it resonated deep in her belly. She'd lived without that sound for over a month. "Hapless?"

"I meant handsome."

"I felt hapless. Helpless. I couldn't stand what I did to you."

For an instant, the enormity of the situation

washed over her and she couldn't breathe.

"Baby?" Logan squeezed her hand harder.

"What can I get you?" A server took a position by their table.

"She'll have hot chocolate. We both will. And a couple of scones. Fruit scones."

"Maybe I wanted coffee." She sucked in air and pushed the horrible memory away as she teased him, trying to be normal.

"You look as though a stiff breeze would blow you away. If you'll take me back, I'm going to take care of you."

She'd thought she could never trust him again. "If … if I thought you'd ever do such a thing again, like at the church—"

"Who would ever have thought it, Victoria? It's nearly beyond belief. I can't in my wildest imagination think of a time when I'd ever be in a position to do what I did. But regardless, it won't matter how many others are involved, if anything like that should happen again. I'd—"

"You'd do the same thing. Because I'd never forgive you if you didn't."

"Can you forgive me now?"

"I can and I do." The relief made her lightheaded and she wanted to lay her head on the table. Was it that easy? "If I wasn't such a damaged person, maybe I'd have listened before—"

"Stop." His adamant tone made her start and stare into his eyes. Eyes filled with compassion and understanding—and love. "I didn't expect anything different, Victoria. How could you not draw the comparison between me and your father? You *were* damaged. Any kid would have been, and I get that you kind of went backward when reminded of that time."

"I went into a tailspin," she whispered, and he blanched.

"You love with that big heart of yours, and I'm so fucking sorry I hurt you."

"Apology accepted." Sincerity rang true in her voice. "We're past it."

"Baby." He put his other hand over their clasped ones, and something cool slipped onto her ring finger. "Your mother sent it to me. With a note. Apparently I was to fix things."

She gave him a tremulous smile before staring down at her ring. "Consider it fixed."

"Two hot chocolate, two scones. You didn't say if you wanted them heated up, but the butter melts easier."

"Thank you." Logan gave his polite smile that concealed his impatience and she hid hers as the server moved away.

"Not the place for a romantic reconciliation," she said, floating free from all the angst and turmoil.

"No, but I missed breakfast staking out your place, and I about froze. So I'm having this scone."

"How long would you have waited out there?"

"For as long as it took. Or until you called the cops. But I was thinking about renting a limo."

She laughed. "Stalking in style?"

"Well, I wasn't giving up. I figured if you kept seeing me and I sent you things it might jog your memory and soften you up. Give me a chance to tell you why."

All those roses, gone who knew where… "Did you think I'd forgotten?"

"I know you, baby. You'd be doing your best to forget you even met me."

There wasn't much to say to that so she sipped

her drink and picked at her scone, giving the bulk of it to Logan. It wasn't easy to eat one-handed, but she accomplished it, because he apparently wasn't relinquishing her other one.

"What now?" He peered at her over his cup. "Can we talk about what your plans are?"

"Later. Right now I'm in dire need of a nap. I haven't been sleeping well and I keep dreaming of some hapless—handsome—prince. You look tired as well."

Logan nearly dropped his cup in his haste to dig out his wallet. Pulling some bills free with two fingers, he let them flutter to the table. Tugging her to her feet, he drew her close and nuzzled her temple. "I'd say your place or mine, but I don't actually have a place."

"What?" She led him toward the door. "Where did you stay last night?"

"A loud, busy place called an emergency room."

She stuttered to a stop. "I thought you said you were okay!"

"I am. Of course, I'm okay. You're here."

She'd see about that when she got him home.

Emilio puffed out his chest when he opened the door for them. Logan gave him a wary look before he squared his shoulders and escorted her inside.

"This is Emilio, Logan. A friend. Emilio, my fiancé, Logan."

Brows nearly up in his hairline, the guard nodded. "Pleasure to meet you, sir. You have a beautiful and wonderful woman in your care."

"I know it. I've always known it."

"Ah." Emilio flashed her a smile. "The impossible has happened, Mizz Sparrow."

"It has." She winked and Logan looked between them. She led the way to the elevator and they stepped inside.

"What was that about?"

"Emilio is a very wise man, Logan. We shared your thoughtful brunch, and he challenged me to step back and think on some things. It led to me standing outside of my building."

"Maybe Emilio would be interested in a job in a warmer climate."

"A full-time job, with benefits, and some time off to spend with his wife and sons."

"We'll figure it out," he promised. "Even if he wants to stay here and freeze."

Logan took a glance around her living space as she removed her jacket. "I love what you've done with it."

His tone was wry, and she knew what he was seeing. A drab, impersonal place, nothing more than somewhere to sleep. She hadn't even unpacked her few keepsakes. "Wait until you see the bed."

With a low sound deep in his chest, he escorted her across the room and into the bedroom. And then he blanked out everything but them.

Drawing her close, he set his lips on hers and the sweetness of the hot chocolate melded with that which was uniquely Logan. Letting him in, he explored her mouth leisurely, but with an underlying sense of desperate need. She pressed her hips against him.

"I'm savoring this," he muttered and stole her breath, his big hands cupping her head again to hold her steady for the sensual assault.

Lost in sensation, her tongue tangling with his, Victoria slipped her arms beneath his jacket and held him tight, her body awakening in remembrance.

"Ow. Geez." Logan stiffened and tore his mouth from hers.

Her fingertips skimming the unfamiliar ridges

along his back, she stepped away. "You're injured! I hurt you. Oh God, Logan." She'd been sidetracked by lust. Deftly unbuttoning his shirt, she was faced with yards of bandage wrap masking most of his muscled chest.

"Just the one side, baby. Well, both, because my right kidney got in the way."

"Let me help you get your jacket off." She eased it down his arms and tossed it on a chair, followed by his shirt. Tenderly drifting her hand over his ribs, she worried her bottom lip.

"It's fine."

"It's not fine." She worked the snap on his jeans free and pulled down the zipper, careful of the firm bulge behind it.

"Uh, Victoria?" Logan was used to being in control in the bedroom, something she preferred, but she was on a mission for her wounded warrior.

"Shush. Let me see." As his jeans sagged to his knees, his black, silk boxers tented beneath her questing fingers, but she moved to study his back. The bandage covered the top of a livid bruise. "Holy crap, Logan. How much does that hurt?" She pressed her lips to the awful mark.

"Not much. And it feels better when you do that."

"This?" She kissed it again and then traced her tongue around the edges.

"That." His graveled tone signaled his arousal, and she teased him for another moment.

"What did the doctor say?"

"Bruised kidney, same for the ribs. I'm a wuss, so I bandaged them. For support."

"You aren't a wuss." She found the tiny metal teeth of the clip securing the bandage and freed it, and then began to unwind the length of fabric. Uncovering the swollen, reddened section, she winced. "Oh, no."

"So I can't belly laugh." Logan stroked her hair.

"What about the kidney?"

"As long as I'm not, uh, showing blood—"

"Blood!" They both winced at her shriek.

"It's okay, baby. It is. Although it'll be a story to tell our grandchildren."

Worried, she studied his face but saw no overt concern. "You'll take it easy. You need to heal up."

"I'd kinda hoped…" He motioned toward the bed.

She set her lips and fit her hand around his erection. It pulsed beneath the silk, another familiar sensation. "Does he still… I mean, can you? With the kidney thing?"

He yanked her against him, grinding his cock against her palm. "Does this feel like he can do it? Besides, I Googled it."

Mirth bubbled in her chest and she allowed it to escape. Logan joined her and then winced.

She shook her head but noted his determination. Kneeling, she unlaced his shoes and eased them off. Working his socks from around his ankles, she slipped them over his toes. Logan had sexy, man toes she loved with a light sprinkling of hair over the knuckles. She loved every part of him. "Step out."

Obediently, he lifted first one foot, then the other, and she set his jeans aside. Glancing up, she marked his bemused stare. "What? I can't take care of you?"

His eyes lit up and he smiled. "I was thinking, seeing as you're down there…"

"Is standing or sitting easier?" She tried to sound stern when her fingers were itching to deal with his boxers.

"I guess sitting. So not the way I envisioned this."

"In sickness and health, darling." Pulling his

underwear down, she pushed gently against his legs and he backed to the bed to sit, the black fabric pooling around his ankles.

Her chest filled with too many emotions to label with Logan here, in the flesh. The bruise on his back and the taping around his ribs had called to her maternal side, except now she was feeling anything but. She knee-walked to him, fitting herself between his thighs and ran her fingernails along their outside. His hair-roughened skin goose-fleshed and his cock jerked.

"I remember this," she crooned, pressing a kiss on his abdomen.

"You missed." His hands gripped the comforter.

"Sorry." She blew a breath of air over his shaft. "Better?"

"Damn it, Victoria. You have too many clothes on," he rasped and then moaned as she fit her mouth over the head, curling her fingers around the base. His hands lifted to feather his fingers through her hair, seeking purchase to direct her movements.

His salty flavor burst over her taste buds as she lapped at him. Inching downward, she sucked until he hit the back of her throat. His thighs trembled as he fought for control and she set out to challenge him. Lashing the notch on the underside with every bob of her head, she drove him higher, his heaving breaths and guttural noises telling her she was successful.

"Baby." Logan tugged at her hair. "If you don't stop—"

Her jaw aching, she redoubled her efforts and he flinched, groaning as he poured himself down her throat. She swallowed frantically, and then let him slip free, resting her head on his thigh.

He stroked her hair. "I wanted to come inside your pussy."

She peered up at him. "I thought after a month apart, your recovery time wouldn't be an issue." A thought struck her, even as he chuckled, and tapped her nose. She said, "Is more than once too often? With the kidney thing?"

"Quit making me laugh!" He held his ribs. "Are you besmirching my manhood?"

"Besmirching?" She giggled. This was the way it was with Logan when he wasn't making her orgasm until she cried uncle. "You should be in the advertising business. For the Medieval Times."

"I'll show you recovery periods." He grabbed her hand and she pushed up to her feet, still laughing. Her t-shirt easily slipped over her head, and Logan shoved the yoga pants down, grunting with satisfaction as her briefs accompanied them. Her bra was a struggle, the hooks resisting his efforts.

"All thumbs?" she teased. "Logan! That was my favorite bra."

He tossed the ruined fabric aside and buried his face against her stomach. The wash of his heated breath gave her the chills and she nearly purred when his hands rubbed down her back to stroke her buttocks. "You smell like home. I've missed this scent."

"Lie back," she murmured.

"I want to touch you."

"I want you to, but get comfortable."

He shuffled backward and stretched out, head raised on the pillows, the double bed dwarfed beneath his frame. She couldn't wait to cuddle with him, although their king-size mattress at home gave them room for antics Logan wouldn't be attempting any time soon.

She knelt beside him and he cupped a breast. "Missed these, too. And this."

The slide of his fingers between her thighs made

her eyes close, the better to concentrate on his touch. His hand pulled back and her hips arched to follow. "Greedy girl. Straddle me."

Carefully, she set a knee on either side of his hips, her wet core grazing his stiffening cock. Her lips twitched.

"Ah, that woman smile."

"Excuse me?"

"The one you give me when you have me exactly where you want me."

"Which is hardly ever, when we're in bed!"

"And the way you like it." Did his voice have a trace of wariness?

"Precisely the way I like it—usually. But today you're mine, although you can follow along the best you're able."

Smirking, he drew her down and lifted up to suck a nipple into his mouth. "Shit." He winced, though tried to hide it.

"I told you. Lie there. You might learn something," she teased.

Rolling his shoulders back, he said, "I'm all yours."

"You are." She fixed him with a hard stare, before leaning to nuzzle the hollow of his throat. His scent was the strongest there and she inhaled deeply before peppering kisses along his neck, then drifting them over his pectorals. His dark nipples peaked, and she darted her tongue across them while grinding her apex against him.

"That feels good," he mumbled.

"I can't wait to do the same thing to your belly when you're not wrapped up like a mummy."

"You could take the bandages all off."

"Now who's greedy?" She traced a pattern over

his heart, and his hand caught hers, pressing it between them, at her apex.

"You're wet, baby."

She'd been ready for him since the moment he'd kissed her. "I want to torture you some more."

"This *is* torture." He humped his hips a little.

Fitting him against her opening, she sank down so his tip slipped inside. Her tissues parted grudgingly and she huffed a breath. It had been a while. Easing back, she pressed forward to take more of him, being filled in that delicious way she shared with Logan.

He set his hands on her hips and facilitated her movements.

"Let me do the work," she whispered, and his hands slipped up her ribcage to hold and stroke her breasts.

Establishing a rhythm, she rode his cock, locking her gaze on his. The connection they'd had, right from the beginning, was still there, and she built on it. With the intimacy, the wounding of her heart healed without a trace, and she made love to him freely.

His chest rose and fell faster, in time with her movements, and one hand left her aching nipple to unerringly find the knot of nerves at her apex. As he worked it, she took him deep, the additional stimulation tumbling her into a shuddering climax. Logan held her steady and groaned his own.

Collapsing on his chest, careful not to stress his ribs too much, she caught her breath, his skin pleasantly damp against her own. He traced her spine her hair. "You still on birth control?"

"Uh, no."

"We'd better get married then, sooner than later."

"I'll need a new dress."

"Whatever you want."

"I want to go home, Logan. To our home."

"I'll take you."

****

Victoria snuggled into the curve of his body, a perfect fit, and he ignored the mild discomfort of his injuries. He'd gladly suffer far worse to have her sleeping so soundly beside him. Her pallor was still worrisome, along with the dark patches beneath her eyes, and she was even thinner without the camouflage of clothing. But he'd take care of her.

He knew she would want to see the completion of her current projects, and he could keep tabs on his business from here, for as long as that took. He wasn't leaving Victoria's side again.

Adrienne could earn her spurs back home, and if she proved herself, he'd promote her. If she would undermine his father, she'd undermine him, but he believed in keeping his enemies close, particularly skilled ones. And he planned to heap so much work on her she wouldn't have time to make mischief.

"Still awake?" Victoria's drowsy voice drew his stare to hers. Her face was slack with sleep—and satiation—and the caveman in his depths pounded his chest. No injury kept Logan Doherty down for long. Speaking of which…

He brushed the tendrils of hair back from her forehead and pressed his hardening cock against her thigh. "Thinking."

Blinking away the cobwebs, her beautiful blue eyes focused. She said, "I can *feel* what you're thinking about. Go to sleep and let yourself heal. We both need a nap."

Watching her drift away again, he relaxed and cleared his mind, slipping into that state he coveted when Victoria shared his bed.

Epilogue

"I think getting married at the beach, with just immediate family suits us better," she said, checking out the venues.

"I'm surprised you've had enough time to come up with any ideas." Logan looked up from his laptop.

"I told you. I'm on top of everything at work and Justin seems perfectly qualified. He's a quick study and Dawna has taken him under her wing." And kicked her out of the nest, to her relief. Logan was mother hen enough, and her mother was calling every day with helpful input.

"He seems competent."

"Jon signed off on him too. Another week or so and I can head back."

He set his computer aside and paced to the windows. "It's going to snow, I bet."

"Not for another month at least. We'll be back long before that, Logan." She stood to join him. The penthouse suite at the luxury hotel was almost overwhelmingly luxurious, but Justin would need the apartment. And Logan wanted a bigger bed. His sore ribs and kidney weren't holding him back, to her immense satisfaction. "I know you're worried about the business."

"No rush. Adrienne is holding the fort and I'm checking in at unpredictable times."

She didn't think she'd like the other woman—on principle—but she wasn't concerned about anything between her and Logan. "Okay. Another few days is all. I have a special project I'd like to finish out." It made her want to grimace, but she'd yet to see the end product.

Logan gave her a strange look and then smiled.

"What?"

"You're beautiful."

"I take it you want something." She ran a fingertip down his throat.

"I always want *that*. With you." He wrapped a long arm around her shoulders and pulled her in.

"Well… I suppose I can fit it in." She nearly blushed at the double entendre and Logan smirked before stealing her breath with one his possessive kisses.

He gently bit her lower lip and soothed the tiny pain with his tongue, before invading her mouth. She pressed closer and gave over to him, transported as always.

The house phone buzzed and they both started. "Ignore it," she suggested.

"I think we'd better answer. Not that we won't pick this up later."

There was a package for her downstairs and a hotel staff would bring it up, according to the reception desk. Victoria went to the door. Within a few minutes, a young man presented her with a padded envelope, and she gave him the tip Logan handed her.

"I thought it was from the office, but it's an address on the other side of town. It looks familiar." She sat at the coffee table and pried the flap open. A hardcover book, about eight by eleven, was cradled by the bubble wrap on the walls of the envelope.

Drawing it out, she caught her breath. Logan sank down beside her and she showed it to him.

"The Tattered Bride."

The image was stunning and evocative. Pride for her creation warred with the reason for producing it. "I … I think it's beautiful."

"And heartbreaking." His voice held a tremor.

"That too." She traced a fingertip along the veil.

"But I had to do it."

"I know, Victoria. I felt you the instant I laid eyes on it. And I'm—"

"Don't." She laid two fingers against his lips and pressed a kiss on them. "We're past it."

Warm breath huffed over her fingers as he sighed, and she drew them down his chin to feather over his jaw.

"Open it."

"I'm not sure. I don't know how to feel about it being a graphic. And I don't think I've ever seen a hardcover graphic. This must be a sample."

"Look and see."

"I don't know. What if it's all exaggerated breasts and blood and gore? Horrible situations?"

"Your choice, baby."

She carefully folded the cover back—and froze. Extremely talented work met her stare, not the trashy style she'd expected. The bride was the only one featured on the page, the background still gray and dreary. But her trained eye noted a few of the rents in the veil were mended, and the soiled gown a little brighter. Even the sad roses appeared a bit perkier.

Turning to the next page, she saw more evidence of repair. The model's face became a trifle less haunted, but only if one looked carefully. "It's a flipbook!"

She pinched all the pages together, letting both covers drop free. With a whirr of paper, she fanned them out in a rapid fashion and the tattered bride became an elegant and radiant image, silhouetted on a background of glowing ivory, her flowers a vibrant red. The color of love. Her heart raced and moisture flooded her eyes. A tear escaped the containment of her fluttering lashes and trailed down her cheek. "It's so beautiful."

Logan smoothed the dampness away, and she leaned into him. Looking at the back of the very last page, she saw it. *All my love, Logan.*

"There's this, too." He handed her a slim circlet set with a comb. Semi-precious gems adorned it in a tasteful pattern, although the silver held a somewhat battered texture.

"My tiara!"

She set it on her head with one hand, laughing when he helped her adjust it, his eyes brimming with love. Still clutching the book, she clambered onto his lap and he wrapped her up. She laid her head against his chest and listened to the beating of his heart, the place where he held her close. Nothing needed to be said, quiet gracing the moment.

The End

www.perielizabethscott.com

THE TATTERED BRIDE

EVERNIGHT PUBLISHING ®

www.evernightpublishing.com

www.ingramcontent.com/pod-product-compliance
Lightning Source LLC
Chambersburg PA
CBHW022034170626
46808CB00003B/1199